The Vam

Illustra

As the lightning hit the statue, it crashed to the ground; unbelievably, a man crawled out from the pieces. Crab-like, he slowly and painfully made his way toward the park bench, a tiny smile playing about his evil, tight blue lips. Forced to live inside a stone statue for three years! It had all been a dreadful mistake. Now he would seek a terrible revenge. Prince Vernon Vampire was out to claim his rightful throne.

ERIC MORECAMBE

The Vampire's Revenge

A Magnet Book

Also by Eric Morecambe in Magnet Books

THE RELUCTANT VAMPIRE

First published in 1983 by Methuen Children's Books Ltd
This Magnet edition published 1984
by Methuen Children's Books Ltd
11 New Fetter Lane, London EC4P 4EE
Reprinted 1985
Text copyright © 1983 Eric Morecambe
Illustrations copyright © 1983 Tony Ross
Printed in Great Britain
by Richard Clay (The Chaucer Press) Ltd,
Bungay, Suffolk

ISBN 0 416 47180 3

Contents

CHAPTER 1

Round the throat a little tightening.
Vernon's back, caused by lightning.

The statue smashed open as the lightning hit it. The life-sized stone statue crashed to the ground and split open from head to toe. If you had been there you would have seen the statue leave the plinth it had been resting on for the past three years. You would also have seen a man crawl out of the broken statue and slowly, very slowly make his way in a crab-like crawl to one of the park benches. He tried to sit on the bench. It took him seven minutes to bend his stiff body into a sitting position.

If you could have got close enough, even with all the pain he was suffering, you would have seen on his very pale face a tiny flicker of a smile playing about his evil, tight blue lips. He was already looking to the

future. He creaked his sore and unused neck muscles and, in obvious agony, they lifted his heavy head to look at the moon through two black and vicious eyes. He worked out the time. It was 2.30 a.m. He thought how lucky he had been.

'I would be dead now if that storm and the lightning had struck in the daytime. We Vampires can't live in the daylight, not for very long.'

Vernon the Vampire was free again. He filled his underworked lungs with the cold night air in the village of Katchem-by-the-Throat in his beloved land of Gotcha, and looked at the smashed stones that had been his home for the past three miserable years.

He allowed his mind to go back to just before he was statued, thinking, 'What a fool I was to allow myself to be turned into stone. After all, it was *my* invention, it was I who was going to turn the others into stone. But soon I will take my rightful place as the Vampire ruler of this country and rule over these stupid peasants as we Vampires have done for almost a thousand years.'

He allowed a small painful smile to invade the corners of his thin lifeless lips. He thought of all his old enemies and the smile widened, causing him more but worthwhile pain.

He thought of his parents, King Victor and Queen Valeeta, whom he now hated, laying some of the blame for his condition well and truly at their door. He thought of his brother Valentine, who was not really his brother, only a step-brother, having been found on the castle steps, and who was not a real Vampire either. He thought of Igon. Oh, how he hated Igon. 'Igon and that stupid so-called brother of mine, they were the ones who put me into that statue for these last three years.' His eyes narrowed as he thought. 'All of them will get the dues they deserve. Each one shall suffer the pain I've suffered and then they shall suffer death.'

Vernon didn't know of the changes in the land of Gotcha, he only remembered the past when the country was ruled by his mother and father. Vernon was still, in his own mind at least, Prince Vernon Vampire, and next in line to be King and ruler of Gotcha.

What Vernon didn't know was that his brother was now the President of Gotcha. His mother and father, the ex-King and Queen, had retired to the country and, although they were still Vampires, lived a normal life. Admittedly they slept in the daytime and stayed awake all night, but they harmed no-one and were popular.

Igon, that was the one Vernon wanted to hurt the most. But Vernon only remembered Igon as he was before he was statued. In those days Igon was the most ugly, the most horrible tiny dwarf with a hump for a back and, as the name suggests, only one eye. He was horrible. But not now, not any more. After Vernon had accidentally turned himself into a statue, Victor and Valeeta abdicated. Victor gave the people of Gotcha a parting gift. Using up all of his Vampire magic, he turned Igon into the most handsome of men. No more the small, wizened, ugly dwarf, but the six foot, very handsome giant.

He also made him into a Prince, Special Prince Igon of Gotcha. But Vernon knew nothing of this. The only thing he knew was hate and how to enjoy it. He sat there on the park bench trying to think of anyone he liked; much to his pleasure, he couldn't.

He rose very slowly from the bench and stayed halfway between sitting down and standing up because he thought he heard a loud creaking noise. He moved again and this time he was sure he heard it. It took several minutes before he realised that it was he who was creaking, having been in that statue for three years in the same position. It was to be expected. He creaked away from the smashed statue, rather like a centipede with rheumatism and made his way to the caves he remembered before he was statued.

As he walked to the hills where the cave was he could feel his strength coming back. After a couple of long slow miles he was beginning to feel better, a lot fitter. He knew his strength was returning to his body, he could feel it. He looked down at himself. His evening dress wasn't in too bad a condition, except that it was covered with three years of dust, but that only needed a brush.

Alas, his top hat was really badly bent; he couldn't wear it even though there was no-one around to see him. To put a squashed top hat on his Vampirian head just wasn't done. The best way to straighten it out would be to fill it with stones and broken bricks. The weight would take the creases out and after a good polish it would look as good as new. This he did.

Of course, he could have magicked it back into shape, but that would be a waste of good magic. At the moment he didn't have the strength to magic anything. Anyway he wasn't going to waste his 'Drac'-given power on a top hat. He was going to save that power and use it on one or two of his old (who wouldn't get much older) friends, the ones who deserved his special way of saying thanks.

After reaching the caves he found the deepest one he could. He knew that after a good day's sleep he would be as fit as he had ever been. The thought kept running through his mind, 'You can't keep a bad Vampire down.' After his sleep he would think about his plans. 'Before the week is over,' he thought, 'Gotcha will be in a state of fear and panic.'

*   *   *

President Valentine rose early that morning, looked out of the window of the Presidential Palace and saw a most beautiful day. Summer was wonderful in

Gotcha. He wondered if the freak storm in the night had done much damage. It had awakened him at about two thirty in the morning and he had had difficulty getting back to sleep. When he did, he had dreamed a terrible dream, a dream that took him back three years into the past. He had seen Igon as he used to be and the old King and Queen, but worst of all he had seen Vernon, who seemed to be smiling. He had smiled all through the dream – a smile frightening enough to frighten the strongest of men. When Valentine awoke he was covered in perspiration.

The sound of the daily paper being squeezed under the bedroom door brought him back to reality. Quickly he picked up the paper and scanned first the headlines and secondly the gossip column. The headlines screeched the words:

PREZ SEZ BIZZ BOOM AT CHRIS

which roughly translated means: 'The President of Gotcha has given much thought to the unemployment situation and feels that, within the next few months, things are bound to improve and, in spite of what people are saying, business will boom before Christmas.'

President Valentine read the page quickly and was quite happy that neither he nor his wife had been misquoted. As he threw the paper on to the bed he made his way to the window, when suddenly he stopped. His eye had caught the words STOP PRESS tucked away in the corner.

He read: 'Last night in a freak storm, lightning hit Vernon statue in park. No sign of Vernon ... 2.30 a.m.' Valentine read the words, 'No sign of Vernon' again and again. A sharp knock on the door broke his concentration.

'Who is it?' he asked.

'Your Secretary of War, General Motors.'

'Come in, Motors,' the President called out. The General entered the room. He was a man of average height and above average width. He tried to salute his President but he was so wide his hand couldn't reach his forehead. It always stopped about nine inches away. He did once go on a diet and his hand actually got to within four inches of his forehead.

'What can I do for you, General? I'm a very busy man at the moment.'

'Sah, hi was wondering, Sah, hif you 'ad read the mornin' pypers, Sah?' he asked. Well, actually he shouted. He shouted everything as if he were still on the parade ground. His wife and children were not only nervous wrecks, but slightly deaf as well.

To give the General his due, he had worked his way up from the ranks of the Gotcharion Army to become their General. The Gotcharion Army consisted of six men, six including the General. At the moment there were two deserters, two on leave and one on manoeuvres.

'Please, General, can you keep your voice down?' the President asked.

'Hov course, Sah,' the General shouted back, the echo making the chandeliers tremble. Valentine shook his head.

'What is it you wish to see me about, General?'

'Well Sah, the late edition hov the mornin' pypers said that the, er, statue hov Vernon had been blown darn, Sah,' the wide General bellowed.

'Yes, I had read that, General, thank you,' the President waved his hand towards the door, hoping that the General just might take the hint.

But the General continued, 'Blown darn, Sah, hand there ain't no sign hov Vernon, Sah. Nah we bofe know that Vernon was put inside the statue, Sah.' The last sentence was spoken in a whisper from the General that could be heard in the next village.

'Please try to keep your voice down, General, I beg you.'

'Hi ham keepin' my voice darn, Sah,' the big General's soft voice once more shook the chandeliers.

'Yes, well I think the best thing you can do,

8

General, is send me a memo.'

He took the General's fat arm and purposefully walked towards the door with him, while at the same time, to show there were no hard feelings, he put an arm around the General's generous shoulder. It reached about halfway between the start of his shoulder and his spine.

'I do appreciate the fact that you thought it necessary to come and see me but please do write to me, eh?'

'Sah,' screamed the General as he saluted his President. His President smiled. The smile faded as he saw a very expensive Ming vase break into little unrepairable pieces.

Once the General was outside the room, Valentine sat down on the edge of the bed. A hundred things went through his mind. He thought about Vernon; about how he had invented a fluid that, with the slightest touch, could turn people into stone; and how he had accidently let some of that terrible fluid drop on himself and he had been placed in the park as a statue. He realized that Vernon would be out to get his own back, not only on him, but on his mother and father and, in particular, Igon whom he hated. He knew that right now Vernon would be in hiding somewhere, planning how to kill them all, and anyone who stood in his way.

* * *

It was dark, very dark in the cave. Vernon opened one eye as he lay on a slab of stone. He knew he was as safe as the Bank of England, which, from the position he was lying in, was West by Nat. West. He allowed himself a grin. Why not? He had slept the reviving sleep of the undead and felt quite strong again.

He had also dreamed a pleasant dream, a dream filled with bare throats, exposed necks and bulging veins just waiting to be bitten. He was hungry now he had rested. The only thing he wanted to do was to satisfy the desire to plunge his teeth into someone.

His black eyes were getting more accustomed to the dark, dank cave. As he swung his feet to the ground he saw a small shape. Heady with the rest and the joy of being alive again, he kicked the small shape. It was his hat, filled with stones and bricks and rocks. When the hat was kicked it didn't travel very far. Had the hat been empty it would *still* be travelling, he had kicked it so hard.

He looked down at his shoe. The pain was awful. For a moment he didn't know whether he still had a toe on the end of his shoe, or even worse, if he still had a toe on the end of his foot. He jumped around the dark cave holding his foot in his hand, screaming vile oaths and swearing old Vampire swearwords like 'Yacoub' and 'Slumpy' and, the most evil swearword of all, (three words really) 'Srettah uoyno emoc'. Those particular words were such naughty swearwords that even Vernon didn't shout them out loud; he only said them through clenched teeth.

He whimpered and limped towards the entrance of the cave. The pain gradually faded away and after a few minutes he was starting to feel his normal unpopular self again as he stood at the entrance of the cave and cursed the world. He stood there and looked at one of Gotcha's special and most beautiful sunsets.

He shaded his eyes as the sun dropped silently behind the distant hills; within seconds it was cool and dark, black dark, Vampire dark. Like all Vampires, he hated sunsets. Sunsets with that great, big, cruel ball of fire hanging in the sky, making the clouds a bright blue and red and pink and green and white and purple . . . 'Horrible,' he thought.

He had once heard about a thing called a rainbow, but, thank Dracula, he had never seen one. Who in their right minds would want to look at lots of colours in the shape of a large bow, hanging in the sky – not doing anything, just hanging there. Now to see a falling star, that was something a bit special, because that meant in Vampire folklore that another Vampire had been born.

He left the cave and made his way to the dusty ribbon of road, carrying his bent top hat, while, with his hands, he brushed away three years of dust from his suit.

He shouted across the fields and trees, 'Watcha Gotcha, I'm here to getcha!' He smiled at the only joke he had ever made in his entire life – if it was a joke.

CHAPTER 2

Igon, Victor, Valeeta the Queen;
All very worried, Vernon's been seen.

Vernon's mother and father, Victor and Valeeta, the ex-King and Queen of Gotcha, opened the curtains the second the sun dropped behind the distant hills and looked out on to a beautiful moonlit night. Victor was always agitated at this time of evening, when he had only just got up. He hadn't even made his coffin yet and making the coffin wasn't a thing he looked forward to. As he refused to make his wife's coffin, she refused to make his, and so they both had to make their own. But, to be fair, the old King did polish both their coffins twice a year. He quite enjoyed doing that; therapy, he called it.

He went to the front door and picked up the paper, *The Nightly Express.* It was lying face down on the mat so he read the back page first. Wilf the Werewolf, a big friend of Victor's and now the manager of Gotcha's football team, had picked the Gotcha team to play Gertcha. Gotcha *v* Gertcha was the match of the season. Victor walked slowly, reading the sports page as he went.

In all probability he would be able to see that game as it was being played at night. Wilf had thought of the idea of playing at night under what he called floodlights; it was a very clever idea and it was typical of Wilf to think of it. Victor thought, 'I've got a lot of time for Wilf.' It was really very simple: at the ground they had installed four huge candles (one at each corner), ten foot thick and sixty feet high, so that on still, clear nights you could see the game.

Of course one or two of the hooligan element tried to stop the game, if their team was losing, by climbing to the top of the candles and blowing them out. But, as they got closer to the flame, the hotter and greasier the candles became, so they soon slid down and were then carted off to the sin bin at the back of the ground. The punishment meted out was short and sharp: the afternoon before the next game they had to reclimb the candles, right to the top, and clean the wick. On the evening of the match they had to climb the candles once again to light them. So hooliganism was down to a minimum.

The only problem with night football was that the game had to be postponed if it was windy, because the wind blew the candles out. A windy summer could cause havoc with the league fixtures.

Victor was reading the sports page as he sat down at the table waiting for his evening breakfast, blood red jelly, a double strength tomato juice and three red black puddings. Valeeta looked at him and the headlines of the paper were facing her:

VERNON'S STATUE SMASHED,
VERNON THE VAMPIRE WAS
NOT ENCLOSED AS THOUGHT.

She snatched the paper out of Victor's hands, leaving him reading empty space. It was quite some seconds before he realised the paper was gone.

With a surprised look still on his face, he said, 'Vot are you doink?'

Valeeta showed him the headlines. 'Look,' she said.

He read them quickly, then again slowly. He looked at his wife and asked, 'Vot does it mean?'

She put the paper down on the table and said, 'If it means what I think it means, then we are in for trouble, all of us.' She picked up the paper and read the article out loud:

'Last night your *Nightly Express* reporter was first on the scene. In our lovely well-kept park, last night's storm in its fury lashed out and hurled down the statue of Vernon the Vampire. As it crashed to the ground it smashed open. Vernon the Vampire was not inside it . . .'

Victor and Valeeta looked at each other.

'Of course he vos,' said Victor.

Valeeta carried on reading:

'If Vernon the Vampire was still alive when the statue was broken into fragments like a cheap mirror on the concrete surround then, in the opinion of the park's spokesman, "He will be on the prowl and he will be out to get those who planned his downfall." When asked if he thought that

15

Vernon would be out to kill the President, the park's spokesman, Mr Spadenfork, nodded his head in agreement saying, "Vernon is still alive 'cos when I've cleaned that statue I'm sure I've seen it breathe, seen it move as you might say.'

Valeeta looked once more at her husband.

'Ivor Spadenfork. He's no spokesman, he's a park attendant,' Victor continued. 'I've known him for years.'

Valeeta smiled, saying, 'It must be over four years, dear.'

'No, I've known him for years, not four years.'

'Darling, how can you have known him four years and then over four years, you silly billy.'

They looked at each other, both thinking, 'You're mad.'

Victor forced a small smile and said, 'Vot else does the paper say, mine orchid petal?'

Valeeta looked down at the paper and found where she had stopped, ahemmed, and carried on:

'It is not the policy of this newspaper to spread fear or panic, but until the Vampire is caught, please keep your children indoors and no-one should venture out between sunset and sunrise. Please do not talk to strangers. The advice of this newspaper is:

If you think you've seen the Vampire Vernon, keep calm and, if he grabs you and starts to squeeze the life out of you, do not fight back, as this could annoy him. If you think he is going to plunge his teeth into your throat then, and only then, scream. If you have a sore throat and can't scream, you must wave your arms about frantically until help arrives.

According to an inside source, the President, when asked if special precautions were being made available to protect the public, said, 'That's very possible.' Once again, I tell the readers of *The Nightly Express*: "Do not panic." '

Valeeta put the paper down. Victor stared across at his wife. They saw fear in each other's eyes. Valeeta thought that Victor would find it very difficult to compete magically with Vernon as he was so out of practice and also completely out of condition – so much so that he became out of breath falling asleep. They slowly and quietly finished their evening breakfast, each with his own thoughts. Victor had silently made up his mind to see his son Valentine, the President. After all, what were friends and relatives in high places for?

*　　　*　　　*

Vernon strolled about Katchem in secret. No-one saw him, he made sure of that. The village was almost deserted, hardly a soul was to be seen, except for the police, and even they were not walking alone as usual, but in sets of eight. Vernon was thrilled that he had caused so much confusion and fear. Considering the fact that Katchem only had eight policemen, Vernon found it relatively easy to avoid the whole of Katchem's police force at once. He walked in and out of the shadows of the streets he knew so well, past Motherscares and Boots the Cobblers.

Fear was beginning to show itself, from the highest person in the land to the lowest.

*　　　*　　　*

In the oblong room at the presidential house Valentine sat with his wife Areta. His young son, Virgil, had been packed off to bed, with a nanny they could trust and a servant to sleep outside the young boy's room. It was the first time Valentine and Areta had seen each other all day as he had been so busy trying to get things planned and organised with regard to Vernon while still running the whole country.

'How did things go, my dear?' she asked with concern in her voice.

'Terrible,' was the quick reply. 'We hardly did anything and ended nowhere. Sometimes I think that the Council and the Senators are all so interested in themselves that they forget about the people who put them there.' He paused and asked the time.

'It's almost nine o'clock.' She held his hand.

'Oh well, I expect Victor and Valeeta will be here soon,' he sighed. 'They will have read the news, and now night has come they will be able to travel, so I think they will be here fairly soon.'

'Why don't you lie down and get some rest before they get here,' she smiled gently at her husband.

*   *   *

Victor and Valentine were almost at the presidential palace and had turned in order to make a good landing as near to the front door as possible. Valeeta made a superb landing, right on the path itself, slowly letting herself to the ground and at the same time powdering her nose. She landed very gently, so gently that she continued walking along the path without one little trip or scuff of her shoes. It was the type of landing that other Vampires would have applauded,

18

a professional's touch.

Victor glided towards the trees in order to get away from what he called 'a cross wind'. He glided rather too quickly and the blustery wind took hold of him, taking him every which way, so much so that as he came into his final approach he had no control at all. He landed, slap, bang, with a heavy wallop into the middle of a large patch of stinging nettles, face down, arms by his side and his legs so crossed that his left leg looked like his right one and *vice versa*. Everything was wrong and against all the rules he had been taught in the V.A.F. (Vamparian Air Force). His top hat was jammed almost over his eyes, squashing the end of his long nose against his top lip, while his Saville Row flying cloak was wrapped around his neck, almost choking him. He did look a sight.

The scream Victor made when he realised he was in a patch of stinging nettles was so loud that it almost made Areta, inside the presidential house, jump out of her skin. Valentine soothed her by telling her that it would be his parents. Within minutes they were all in the oblong office greeting each other.

Areta watched as Valentine held his mother by the throat as gently and as softly as a breeze, a sure sign of Vamparian affection. Victor also looked on, smiling his approval.

'What was that noise I heard out there?' the President asked politely.

'Who else but your father? He made a terrible landing in a rather large patch of nettles. Lucky for him that your guards were there to help him out. Anyway, it serves him right.' She looked at her husband as if to say, 'I love you, but you are a fool.'

Victor thought it was time to defend himself. 'Ya. It vos the cross vind, it vent across me.' They all looked at him as he started to scratch and blow on an angry-looking nettle rash.

'Cross wind, my eye teeth,' Valeeta said. 'You are an old fibber,' she added, with a tiny amount of affection. 'It was because you are carrying too much weight. Since you retired from being King, you have put on at least a stone and a half in weight. Just look at that belly.' They all looked where she was pointing and saw a shirt that was stretching over a larger area than it was made for and, here and there, quite a lot of exposed pink tummy, which was beginning to look like expertly blown bubble gum.

'Vot you are sayink is a lie. Never am I puttink on a stone ant a half in veight, never. An ounce or two, maybe.'

'An ounce or two, an ounce or two. What rhubarb you talk. Who was it who couldn't tie his shoelaces when he got up this evening, because he couldn't bend over? Who had to tie them for him? Me!' The ex-Queen had a smug look on her face. Victor looked down at his shoes, but he couldn't see them for his tummy. He looked back at his family and with his eyes asked them all if he was too plump and overweight. They all nodded with a smile. It was the first time Valentine had smiled that day.

Valentine was the first to broach the subject of Vernon by saying, 'I'm glad you could both be here. I take it that you have read the papers?'

'Ve only get the von, *The Nightly Express*.'

'Well, that paper carried the story about ... you know who.' He looked away from the old King and

Queen. He knew how upset they both must be. After all, Vernon was their son. Valeeta was sitting in a straightbacked chair with her husband standing behind her. They looked very regal.

The Queen was the first to speak, 'Yes, my dear, we saw the paper and that's why we are here. We've talked it over, your Father and I, and we feel that we would like to help you to ... er ... get ... have ... er ... Vernon put away for a, well a long time ... maybe for ever,' she was finding it difficult to speak. 'Or better still, out of the country altogether, deported, I think they call it.'

When the Queen had finished speaking there was a silence. The only movement in the room was Victor, scratching his nettle rash. Valentine walked round the large room before speaking. He stopped and looked directly at the only two parents he had ever known, two Vampires. They had found him and they had reared him. What he was about to say could be hurtful and difficult.

'I have to be honest with you both. I don't think that deporting Vernon, or even putting him away for a long time is the right thing to do.' He held his hand up to stop what was going to be an interruption from the Queen. She stiffened a little, not being used to having to be silent. But, after all, she was an ex-Queen and Valentine was the President. 'Please let me finish,' Valentine asked.

'Ya, let him finish,' Victor nodded his consent for Valentine to carry on.

'Thank you, Father. I don't think putting him away or sending him to another country, well, is really enough. What I'm trying to say,' he started to speak slowly, 'what I'm trying to say, or what I think should be done ... er, what I'd like to see happen ... what I'm trying to say without hurting your feelings, is that I think, well, that maybe we ... I think maybe ...'

Areta spoke for the first time. She was blunt and went straight to the point that Valentine was finding difficult.

'He will have to be killed,' she said in a firm voice. 'That is what the President was trying to say. Vernon should be killed. We both know that Vernon is your son and you will naturally want to try and help him. I would do the same for my little boy, your grandson. That is understandable. But we all know that Vernon is a maniac and, if something isn't done, will kill. He would have no compunction in killing you too, or me, or Valentine, or even your grandson ... He can't forgive and he will never forget. A stake must be put through his heart.' She stopped talking and felt they must all be able to hear her heart beating. She was shaking with fear and anger. Valentine walked over to her.

'Thank you, darling,' he said. He then looked at the only parents he had ever had and said, 'My wife is right. That's what I was trying to say.'

There was a long silence. No-one moved, even Victor had stopped scratching. It was Victor who broke the silence with a rather loud 'Ahem' which he followed with, 'Ya, maybe you are right.'

The ex-Queen looked more than sternly towards him. He saw the look and said, 'Maybe not, I don't know. Vot do you think, mine little crocus?' He smiled at his wife and scratched the back of his hand. The ex-Queen was much more definite than her husband.

'He is my son. Mine and Victor's. For the past three years Victor and I have been very happy living in the country, but our son Vernon, he has suffered; not you, Valentine, nor you, Areta, nor Victor or I, but our own son, Vernon. He was inside that statue for three years. Can you imagine what that must have been like, not being able to move? Only to be able to look at what was going on around him? Never being able to blink, let alone speak?

'Certainly he won't forgive and definitely he won't forget but I will not believe that he would harm, let alone kill, one member of his family. We are his family. We should be out there looking for the poor boy to help him, not just saying "let's kill him." That is the easy way. He is part of a dynasty. He comes from a thousand years of Vampires, pure Vampire stock. He is the last of the true Vampires; he should be helped. Have you forgotten what your father did for this country? Have you forgotten what your father did for Igon? He turned him from a twisted, horrible, bent thing into the most handsome of men. That was Vampire magic, great Vampire magic. Magic that took every ounce of strength your poor father had.

Victor nodded and scratched.

'I know that both physically and mentally your father is no match for Vernon any more. He gave everything that he could for the benefit of you and this country. Vernon would do the same. I have to agree that something must be done, but I will fight to the end to see that our poor little son is not skewed.* Where is my poor little boy now? Probably huddled

* Vampirian word for death by the stake

24

in some dirty old barn crying for his Mummy, me . . .' She wiped her eyes, although there were no tears as Vampires can't and don't cry. But at that particular moment she was a little confused.

'I am against the killing of my son Vernon and that is final. Come, Victor, we will try and find our confused and bewildered boy who wouldn't harm a fly.'

'Mine dear, I'm agreeink with all you sayink, but can't ve haff one little drink before ve go, ya?'

'No, you can't. You have just started your diet.'

*   *   *

The confused and bewildered little boy was hiding in the doorway of an unlit shop writing in a notebook. He wrote: 'Igon first, Valentine second, King Victor third and Queen Valeeta fourth. All to be removed, but tortured first. Not necessarily in that order.'

CHAPTER 3

The Inspector tries to clear up the case.
Vernon soon puts him in his place.

Special Prince Igon was on a business trip to Gertcha. Having concluded his business, which was getting Gertcha to buy nuts from Gotcha, he had booked his seat home on the new fancy stage-coach, the *Gertcha-gotcha Flyer*. The coach, an eight-seater, pulled by the best six horses from both lands, was the very latest in style and had all the latest safety devices, including disc hooves on the back two horses.

Although the driver and his co-driver sat outside on top of the coach, they shared one enormous hat. It had two skull caps covered with one long piece of material, rather like a plank of wood with two inverted soup bowls. The idea was that it would keep the rain off both of them at the same time.

Inside the coach was a very pretty stewardess serving drinks and duty free tobacco. The trip itself was very quick considering the distance covered; over two hundred miles in just over ten and a half hours, twenty-four horses, a change of driver and co-driver, three stops and four different (but all very pretty) stewardesses, all of whom fell in love with Igon.

Igon sat by the window looking out into the darkness. He had bought his duty free drinks and tobacco, although he didn't smoke or drink. He had bought them for the old folks' home on the outskirts of Katchem. He felt sorry for the old folks and had taken them under his wing. He stared into the night, but his thoughts were on the rumours about Vernon and a storm.

'Have you heard?' said one passenger to another.

'Heard what? the other passenger asked.

'What happened in Katchem.'

'No, what?'

'They had a storm last night and the statue was blown down.'

Igon was only half listening to the conversation, as he was working out on his portable abacus how much money he had made for his country with his nut deal.

'What statue?' the second passenger asked.

'Just a moment, are you a Gert or a Got?' the first passenger asked.

'I'm a Gert,' the second passenger said with a certain pride.

'Oh well, in that case you won't understand,' the first passenger said, as he continued to play with a multi-coloured cube, trying to get squares of the same colours on each side of the cube.

'Why won't I understand?' asked the second passenger in a small hurt voice.

'Because you are a Gert and not a Got. If you were a Got, you would understand about the statue.'

'What should I know about it?' the second passenger almost begged. 'It might help me with my business deal in Gotcha.'

'What business are you doing in Gotcha, then?' asked the Got man.

'I'm going there to sell nuts to the Gots,' the second man said.

'Why?' asked the Got man.

'Because they've sold all theirs.'

Igon had started to eavesdrop when he heard the words 'nuts' and 'business'.

'So please tell me about the statue that's been blown down?'

'Well, it's called the Vernon statue,' the Got man confided. 'It was blown down in a storm last night and Vernon wasn't in it.' He looked at the Gert man through half a wink and then went back to his cube. The Gert man looked nonplussed.

'I don't understand,' he said. 'He wasn't in it?'

'I said you wouldn't,' replied the Got man.

'Well, may I ask,' the Gert man said, smiling sarcastically, 'if, when you put up a statue of someone in Gotcha, do you always put him inside the statue?'

Igon tapped the Got man on the shoulder before he could answer, and asked, 'Did you say the Vernon statue, the one in Katchem?'

'Yes,' the Got man nodded. 'It blew down last night.'

'And Vernon was in it?'

'Are you a Got?' asked the Got man.

'Yes,' replied Igon.

'No, Vernon wasn't in it.'

'Not in it?' said the incredulous Igon.

The Got man whispered loudly towards Igon, 'They say he escaped and is after revenge.' The Got man looked at Igon this time through two half-closed eyes while at the same time nodding slowly.

Meanwhile the Gert man, who had understood not one word of the conversation, thought he would change the subject by asking Igon, 'What business are you in, young sir?'

'Nuts,' Igon replied and after that remark the conversation seemed to peter out.

Igon turned his head back to the window and looked out into the blackness. His eyes focused on the two eyes looking back at him from his own reflection. They were full of fear. As the coach moved along towards Gotcha he felt a shiver run through his body, but it wasn't a shiver of cold. Igon was frightened, and he knew it. His thoughts were filled with Vernon.

*　　　*　　　*

A new chief inspector of police was brought in to take over the 'Vernon Problem' and to make sure that

Vernon was caught and punished. His name was Chief Inspector Speekup. Unfortunately he was very deaf, a result of never having dried his ears properly after washing when he was a little boy. At the moment he was busy with the men in the Katchem Police Force, working out how to combat the Vernon Problem. Twenty tall candles had been lit in order, as the Inspector put it, to throw more light on the case. All leave had been cancelled. His team of eight men looked at him with white faces and nervous eyes. He spoke.

'Men,' he snapped, as he looked at his eight policemen. 'We have been chosen.' He was pressed to perfection in his light brown uniform, his pointed dark brown hat and a cream shoulder cape. He looked like a chocolate cornetto.

'We have been chosen to apprehend the vicious Vampire, Vernon, and bring him to justice.'

The fear in the men's eyes grew because they all knew that the Inspector had never caught a criminal in his entire career with the force. He was the joke of the Gotcha police, the joke being, 'Chief Inspector Speekup couldn't catch his pants on a nail'. And now here he was after the worst type of criminal, a criminal who had magic on his side, who could escape from anywhere and who couldn't die unless he was killed in a special way. They all thought the same thing: 'Fat chance we've got of catching Vernon with this fancy-dressed idiot leading us...'

'And I want him,' he continued. 'I want him here in my prison and I want him soon.' His voice was as dry as a packet of salty crisps. He clicked his heels together.

'I know what you want,' was heard quietly from the back line of men. But the Inspector didn't hear it. He only saw all his men smiling.

'That's it, men,' he said. 'That's what I like to see – men who smile in the face of adversity.' The men began to shuffle their feet. 'That's it, men,' he said again. 'Keen to get on with it, eh?'

His dry voice took on the sound of a file rasping against iron. He laughed, a rather throaty laugh, like four dice shaken in a tin box. 'Now, before we go out and get this man, nay, this fiend, are there any questions?'

'Where do you think he is, Sir?' asked Number Six.

'Pardon?' the Inspector said, putting his hand to his ear.

'Where do you think Vernon is?' Number Six asked again.

'Yes, very good, very good, yes do that,' the Inspector said, looking at Number Four.

'Do what, Sir?' Number Six asked yet again.

'Well, that's possible,' the Inspector said, this time looking directly at policeman Number Three. 'Are there any more questions? Come along now, you mustn't be afraid of me just because I'm an officer.' Out of the corner of his eye, he saw a hand raised by Number Seven. 'Yes, what is the question?' he grinned.

'May I ask whether you heard the first question or not ... Sir?'

The Inspector allowed his grin to widen before he spoke.

'I would say between now and midnight,' he said, taking out a large pocket watch and showing it to the men. 'Good question that. I only hope all you other men are as quick and perceptive as that man there.' He pointed to policeman Number Two. 'Right, if that's all you want to know, off you go, as I have work to do. I'm working on a plan.'

The rest of the policemen all looked at each other in an embarrassed way and filed out of the Inspector's office. Only Sergeant Salt remained behind. When they were completely alone and the door had been closed the Sergeant spoke.

'Excuse me ... Sir ... Sir ... Inspector, Sir ... Excuse me, Sir.'

The Inspector was busy looking at a street map and didn't seem to hear, so the Sergeant tapped him on the right shoulder.

The Inspector jumped three feet into the air with fright. When he came down he looked at the Sergeant with a sickly grin and said in a voice as dry as autumn leaves, 'What can I do for you Corporal?'

'Sergeant, Sir,' the Sergeant beamed proudly.

'Pardon?'

'Sergeant, Sir. I'm a Sergeant, Sir.'

'Good idea, no sugar in mine.'

The Sergeant slowly left the room and the Inspector was left alone in his office.

The Sergeant was the last man out of the station. All the other men had gone away in a group, a very close group, all believing in that old saying, 'safety in numbers'.

From the police station steps, the Sergeant looked up the road, along the road and down the road. It was empty, not a soul in sight. He took a deep breath and walked down the station steps on to the street itself. Although a reasonably brave man, for the first time since he was a little boy, he felt scared of the dark. There was not a light to be seen. He walked as close to the railings as he could. He looked up at the closed curtains of the Inspector's office.

'He'll be in there,' the Sergeant thought, 'wondering when his tea will be brought in.'

The Sergeant had gone about twenty nervous feet when he suddenly dropped to the ground. He had tripped over something. He was unhurt and jumped up as quickly as he could. In the darkness he groped with his hands on the ground hoping to find what had tripped him up. He soon found it. It wasn't very nice. With many years experience behind him, he knew the second he touched it, that he had tripped over a body.

He looked round in the hope that there might be someone walking along who could give him a hand. But of course there was no-one. He even thought of shouting for the Inspector, but then thought better of it. If the Inspector couldn't hear him when they were in the same room, what chance did he have of hearing him when he was out of the room?

So, alone, with a tremendous effort, he slowly dragged the body back to the police station, up the steps and into the hall. The body was quite dead. He undid the cravat from around the poor man's neck and saw two tell-tale punctures in the man's throat. Vernon had struck.

*　　　*　　　*

Vernon walked away into the darkness as he saw the policeman lift the body into the station. He wiped his

lips with a red spotted handkerchief and smiled an evil smile. He had struck because he thought it was time to prove to one and all that he meant business, and doing it right outside the police station showed the contempt he felt for the police force. It was unfortunate for the victim, but Vernon hadn't given him a single thought. As the man had come towards the police station out of the darkness, Vernon had sprung forward like a panther and plunged his teeth into him with vicious power.

*   *   *

The Sergeant went into the Inspector's office without knocking, knowing that if he did knock it would be a waste of time. The draught from the open door made the flame of the candle on the Inspector's desk flicker, otherwise the Chief wouldn't have looked up.

'There's a body outside and it's dead, Sir,' the Sergeant said, with as much control as possible.

'Well, it's about time, and no sugar in mine, please.'

It was then that the Sergeant realised that this was going to be a long night. He walked out of the office and, with strong powerful arms, picked up the body and carried it into the office.

The Inspector was looking out of his office window and didn't hear the Sergeant enter his room. The Sergeant knew that he wouldn't be able to attract the Inspector's attention just by talking or making a noise, so he put the dead man in the chair in front of the Inspector's desk. He stood behind the poor unfortunate man, while he held him in a sitting position.

The Inspector turned round and looked at the Sergeant and then at the body sitting in the chair. He did this three times before he spoke.

'Well, aren't you going to introduce me to the gentleman, Sergeant?'

The Inspector came round the desk, arm outstretched to shake hands with the dead man.

Sergeant Salt drew a deep breath and shouted, 'Sir, this man is dead.'

'Hello, Fred,' the Inspector said with a smile. 'I'm pleased to meet you.' He held out his hand and watched as the body slowly sank off the chair on to the floor.

'Good Lord, the man has fainted.' He knelt down by the body and said, 'Sergeant, help me put his head between his legs. Got to get the blood flowing to his head.'

The Sergeant knelt with him. 'Sir, can't you see the man hasn't fainted. The man has been bitten by Vernon.'

'Oh yes, good idea, I should have thought of that. Where is it kept?'

The Sergeant jumped up quickly and went to the desk. He picked up a quill pen and wrote 'HE'S DEAD'.

He showed the note to the Inspector who read it, looked at the Sergeant and said, 'Come now, Sergeant, that's not the way to spell Fred.'

The Sergeant quickly undid the cravat, and showed the Inspector the two small punctures on the man's neck. A slow but genuine realisation came over the face of the deaf Inspector. He looked at the marks on the neck, then at the man's face he was holding in his arms. The Inspector threw the head away from him with such force that if the poor man had not been dead already he would have been then.

'This man is dead, Sergeant.'

The Sergeant nodded his head, picked up the paper with the message on it and rolled it into a funnel. He stuck the sharp end into the surprised Inspector's ear and shouted at the top of his voice, 'Vernon.'

The Inspector went two different colours, neither of them very pretty. He ran round the office shouting, 'Police, Police!'

Sergeant Salt left the office the same way as he had arrived, carrying the unfortunate man. Once outside the office, he closed the door with his foot and gently laid the man on a bench in the hall. He stayed there for the next few minutes and watched the Inspector open the office door slightly and, with rather wide eyes in a very pale face, close it again. He did this seven times.

CHAPTER 4

A wizened old crone gives Igon a warning.
'Twelve hours from now you may be in mourning'.

Vernon felt good and full of life. The magnificent seven policemen were patrolling the centre of every main street in Katchem.

*　　　*　　　*

Igon sat silently in the rocking stage-coach, thinking hard.

*　　　*　　　*

The President sat with his First Lady in the presidential house and worried.

*　　　*　　　*

Victor and Valeeta were having a row. Because he

40

was so over-weight he was flying too low and kept hitting the branches of the trees.

*　　　*　　　*

Things were going Vernon's way. He took off and flew towards Bloodstock Castle, high on the hill; the castle he had lived in with Victor and Valeeta, his brother Valentine and, of course, Igon. How could he forget Igon? He was number one on his hit list.

*　　　*　　　*

Special Prince Igon looked back into the stage-coach, after staring into the blackness of the countryside. He spoke to the pretty stewardess.

'How many hours, do you think, before we get to Katchem?'

'Not long now, Sir, maybe another two hours, three at the most,' she simpered. 'We'll pick up speed again when we change horses and drivers at the next changeover stop, a place called Watchit. We'll get a good meal there – well, we should, it's a Trust House Twenty.'

The coach went over a large stone and threw her forward, almost into his arms. She blushed the colour of a glass of port. She seemed in no hurry to get back. Even through her embarrassment she stayed close to Igon. He, being a gentleman, apologized for the coach going over the stone. She, being a lady, accepted the apology. She carried on talking.

'I have heard there have been some severe storms and some flooding near Katchem, but I don't know for sure.' She giggled as she sat back on her own seat.

A very old lady in the corner of the coach, who

41

hadn't spoken to anyone the whole trip, even when they had stopped to change drivers and horses, put her hand out and gently touched Igon on his arm.

'Forgive an old lady, Sir, but aren't you Igon?'

'Yes, I am, old lady,' he said with a pleasant smile.

'*The* Igon?'

'Pardon?' asked a surprised Igon.

'Are you the Igon who used to live at Bloodstock Castle? The Igon who was changed from an ugly-looking horrid thing into what you are now, a handsome and rich prince?'

The pretty stewardess lowered her eyes and at the same time coyly fluttered her eyelashes. The other people in the coach looked at Igon as if he was now something different, which of course he was.

Igon tried to avoid the inquiring looks. He held the old woman's hand and said gently: 'Well, not rich, and not really a prince for that matter and as for handsome, well, I don't really think that, er, I, er ...' His conversation fluttered to a stop, as the stewardess's eyelashes carried on fluttering, seeming as if they would never stop.

'A lot more handsome than you were, eh?' the old woman crackled.

'Well, yes I, er, suppose so,' he answered softly and nervously. He loosened her arm from his own.

She grinned. 'I hear that Vernon has escaped from the statue.'

It was direct and heard by all in the coach. Even the wheels seemed, for that sentence, to stay quiet.

'Oh really,' he said in a dry cracked voice. 'Maybe it's a rumour.' The corners of his mouth twitched with uncontrollable tiny nerves.

'Oh no, Sir, it's no rumour, I can assure you. An old crone like me knows a rumour when she hears one. Vernon has escaped and that's the truth.' She laughed throatily, with a sound like fifty whips being cracked.

'Your hand, Sir, may I look at your hand. No charge, not even half a rem.' She took his hand in hers before he could answer yes or no. She held it open and looked hard at it. Igon felt something akin to fear run through his body.

'Do not be afraid, young sir. I'm sure that no harm will come to you, at least not tonight. Oh no, not tonight.'

'Thank you. At least that's a comforting thought.' He tried to sound brave.

She held his hand with the strength of a bear. 'You will meet someone tonight whom you won't recognise because you can't see him, but he'll talk to you. No, my Prince, no harm will come to you tonight . . . but tomorrow,' she looked at the fear in his eyes, 'tomorrow, well, that could be different, couldn't it? Who knows what the future holds?'

She dropped his hand and leaned back in the corner. He noticed that everybody in the coach was very silent, trying to look as if they hadn't heard a word, but Igon knew they had.

'An old woman prattling,' Igon told the coach. He looked across at the old lady, whose piercing eyes were still fixed on him. He closed his eyes but he knew that he wouldn't sleep that night.

*　　　*　　　*

Vernon arrived at the castle. Iron bars had been put

43

up at every window. Every door was locked and bolted. No-one could have got inside, except maybe Vernon. He flew round the castle once and came to rest at the castle entrance. He walked to a sign hanging on the huge castle doors. He read:

BLOODSTOCK CASTLE CLOSED.
ALL ENQUIRIES AT THE POLICE STATION.

VALENTINE. PRESIDENT.

Vernon read it three times before he thought he understood it. *President!* Valentine was President. But President of what? A bank, maybe? It went through his mind over and over again. 'President Valentine. President Valentine. President Valentine. Then there is my mother and father – and Igon. Where's Igon? Where is he?'

He read the sign again. "All enquires at the police station." He took off quickly, heading for the village, and the police station in particular.

Vernon flew back to the village non-stop. He was feeling so exhilarated that, for the first time in the history of flying, he did something that had never been attempted before by anyone, bird or Vampire: aerobatics. He zoomed up and down, along and close to buildings, cattle and trees. He found the pure feeling of freedom.

It was on that trip that he performed the first ever loop the loop; that is, a loop inside another loop. He was doing one very large loop, not thinking of doing another, when suddenly, at the peak of the first loop, his top hat fell off. While he was looking heavenwards, his hat was tumbling earthwards. Vernon put his

hands together, straight out in front of him, like a diver diving from a great height. This gave him the extra speed that he needed. He caught up with the hat and snatched it, while at the same time he zoomed upwards, back towards the heavens. All this was done inside the first loop he had already done. Of course it wasn't called loop the loop in those days. It was known as catching the topper.

Vernon glided to the centre of the village, with his arms spread out and the wind billowing his cloak. His highly-polished patent shoes flicked first to the left and then to the right, guiding his body to the place of touchdown opposite the police station.

He was so in control of himself and his flying, that he resolved to land on one foot. A one-footer was very difficult to do without a hop or a skip after touch-down. The wind, or what little there was, seemed to keep out of his way. He had never done a one-footer before. Very few Vampires had. Vernon seemed to remember that his uncle Varicous had done it – but he had to because he only had one leg anyway.

Vernon felt very confident and somehow knew that the Great Drac himself was on his side. He came in for the one-footer, his heart pounding four to the dozen. He landed with perfect precision on the flags of the pavement, a one foot landing with the toe of his shoe fitting right into the join of the four paving stones. He felt very proud of himself. So much so that he looked up at the sky, tipped his top hat and shouted to the Great Drac, 'Follow that, kiddo!'

Vernon had been there, opposite the police station, no more than one minute when he looked up the long, dusty road. He saw his mother, ex-Queen Valeeta, come in for an almost perfect female landing; that is to say, she landed on both her high heels at once and in no way did she allow her ankles to lean over either to the left or to the right.

A small puff of dust exploded beneath her feet as she came to a halt, right in the middle of the main street. She stood still for two seconds, then wiped her left shoe on the back of her right leg, followed by her right shoe on the back of her left leg. After looking down to check that her shoes were clean again, she raised her eyes and looked along the metaphorical landing strip that her husband Victor was about to come in on.

From the shadows, Vernon watched his father with eyebrows raised in disbelief. 'This,' he thought, 'is the man who holds the oldest and least endorsed of all Vampire flying licences.'

Victor came in on a wing and a Drac prayer:

Oh great and mighty Drac
Please don't let me land on my back.

Vernon had only ever flown with the élite 'Crazy Bat Squadron' whose motto was: 'Reach for the Throat', and he felt ashamed, but not sorry, as he saw his father come in for a landing that could have been done better by a three-month-old Vampire. It was the first time he had seen anyone land on his stomach. It was a three point landing, Vernon thought: chin, stomach and toes.

The ex-Queen waited with resigned tolerance for her husband to get back on to his feet. As he did, he gave her an embarrassed shrug of his shoulders. She looked at him, then away from him, as she flicked his bow tie straight, expelling a heavy breath that seemed to say, 'Oh dear'. Vernon kept well in the shadows not wanting to be seen by them, nor anyone for that matter.

Victor and Valeeta, unknowingly watched by their son and heir, entered the police station to ask Sergeant Salt if he had any news about Vernon. Sergeant Salt looked up from the report he was writing about the poor deceased man who was lying on a bench not more than three feet away. The ex-King held back the ex-Queen as they made their way to the desk.

'Gutt Evenink,' Victor smiled and flourished his hat in the style of a conjurer about to make the whole world disappear. 'Hi ham the ex-Kink Victor, ant this is mine ex-Queen Valeeta.'

The Sergeant looked at the ex-Queen and said,

'Good evening Madam, is there anything I can do for you?' He was as nice as he could be. He knew that they were Vampires almost on probation. He also knew that they were the parents of the wicked Vernon who had almost definitely killed the man lying on the bench. But he knew that they were not to know that as yet.

The ex-Queen, putting on her best smile, softly said, 'Have you seen anything of my son since the statue fell down?'

'Yah,' added Victor. Then, looking at the man on the bench he added, 'Drunk?'

'No, dead,' the Sergeant said quietly.

'Dead drunk?' Victor laughed out loud, a sound reminiscent of a man being choked to death.

'No, Sir, not drunk, just dead,' the Sergeant answered.

Victor stopped laughing and asked, 'Kilt?'

'Yes, you could say that.' The Sergeant looked hard at them both.

'Please,' the ex-Queen butted in. 'Have you seen my son, Vernon?'

'How vos this man kilt?' persisted Victor.

'Oh, I'll show you, Sir. I'll show you, all right?' The Sergeant moved round his desk and quickly made his way to the dead man. He moved the unfortunate man's cravat, exposing the two puncture marks in his neck.

'That was how he was killed, Sir.' Sergeant Salt said, leaning a little heavy on the sarcasm.

'With a fork?' asked Victor.

'No, Sir,' the Sergeant said slowly and deliberately. 'Not with a fork, but with teeth.' He pointed to his own teeth. 'With teeth maybe a little longer than mine.'

'How lonk has he been kilt?'

'What?' The Sergeant's temper was beginning to show a little.

'How lonk has he been kilt? Is he a long time kilt?'

'I'm not too sure. Maybe an hour, maybe a little less, I don't know.' The Sergeant was getting tired. He had had a long day and now it was going to be a long night.

The ex-Queen was drumming her long fingers on the desk top. 'I have no wish to be rude, but could you please tell me, have you seen Vernon or heard from him?'

The Sergeant spoke very softly but with a firmness that insisted on your attention: 'No Madam, I have not seen or heard from Vernon. But there is one thing you can be sure of,' he pointed to the man on the bench, 'he has.'

'Leaf this to me, mine little royal relish,' Victor said, realizing the Sergeant was about to lose his temper. He smiled in the direction of the law, as he said: 'Now, mine fine policeman frent . . .'

The Inspector's door opened and shut again very quickly.

Victor asked, 'Whom vos that?'

'The Inspector.'

'Yah,' the old King said. Then changing his tone of voice, he said, 'Right. First of all, you must pick up the man on the bench ant hold him hup on his feet, yah?' The Sergeant looked puzzled as Victor continued, 'Please, you must trust me. Vot I'm going to do, I'm doink for the best.'

This time the ex-Queen interrupted. 'You are not thinking of doing the B.H.B.T.L., are you?'

She sounded perturbed more than angry. Victor only nodded.

The Sergeant asked, 'What's a B.H.B.T.L.?'

'Bring him back to life,' Victor answered with a broad smile.

'But can you do such a thing?' asked the incredulous Sergeant.

'No he can't,' snapped the ex-Queen. 'And the reason he can't is very simple. He hasn't got enough magic power left in him. One has to be supremely fit to attempt a B.H.B.T.L.'

'Yah, you are right, mine little vol-au-vent. But, as you keep sayink, I am only half fit. Now you, mine little madrigal, are very fit. At least a gut three-quarters fit. Yah? So now then, if ve combine our strengths ant our powers, then ve will be a gut one ant a quarter fit, yah?'

The ex-Queen and the Sergeant looked at the man on the bench, then to the old King, then to each other.

'Can it be done? Can the two of you B.H.B.T.L.? Him?' the Sergeant started to get quite excited.

Valeeta looked deep in thought as she said, 'Well, there's no reason why not. But it's never been done that way before. Yet I see no reason why at least it shouldn't be tried. Power is power and magic is magic.' She looked at her husband asking, 'Do you think you can remember what to do? And can you still go into the trance, the deep one I mean?'

'Of course, mine little mahatma. I go into a trance every time I look at your beautiful face, mine little daughter of Dracula.'

'I hope you haven't been drinking, Victor.'

'Ven? How? Vere? Ant besides, you said I ham on a diet.' He chucked her under her chin.

'What do you want me to do?' Sergeant Salt asked.

'Please, mine policeman frent, pick the man up ant put him into a standink position, yah?'

That done, Victor went into a small dance, the Vampire Trance Dance. The dance was specifically to ask the Vampirian gods to let the dead man be released from the unhappy haunting grounds.

Valeeta sang in a soprano voice, so high that only Vampire gods and Vampire dogs could hear her.

Oh my Drac, get out of the sack.
Can you give us what we lack?
Can you give us what we lack?
We lack what you can give us,
can you give this man the Shivers?
(She pointed to the dead man)
Nic Nac Paddy Wac, give a man a bite.
This old man seems quite all right.
Hack heck hock,
Hick hike hook.

The Sergeant held the man as straight as he could. He watched as Victor suddenly started to float above the desk. He watched as smoke came out of his ears. Red smoke. The red smoke whirled around the room and around the dead man's ears. The Sergeant saw the red smoke actually enter the dead man's ears, and his hand, the one over the dead man's heart felt a slight bump from inside the body he was holding. A

51

few seconds later he felt another one.

The ex-Queen was now also floating with her husband. They seemed to be dancing a waltz, but a waltz about two feet off the ground. Another heartbeat followed by another, then another, only this time stronger than the ones before. Thump, thump, thump. Three in a row. The man the Sergeant was holding seemed to be getting lighter.

The office door opened as Inspector Speekup came bravely out to give his orders. He saw a smile on the dead man's face and two people in full evening dress waltzing two feet above the ground. He saw his Sergeant crying with happiness and relief. That was when he left the world for a few fainting seconds.

The Sergeant could see the strain on the faces of Victor and Valeeta, who were oblivious to all around them. The colour was slowly coming back into the face of the once-dead man. He was now 'not fully dead'. An eye flickered in the faces of both the dead man and the Inspector. They opened their eyes at the same moment.

The Inspector was the first to speak. He looked at the cheerful corpse and said, 'Aren't you dead?'

The reborn man shook his head and with a smile said, 'No, I'm Fred.'

'Pardon?' asked the Inspector.

'That's right,' said the happy, smiling man, 'Garden, Fred Garden.'

Victor fell heavily to the floor from around four feet up. His work over, he was almost too tired to rise from the sitting position he was now in. He did manage to say that the newly-born man would be slightly deaf for a little while.

The ex-Queen floated gently down to the floor with the words, 'By the Drac, I'm hungry. Expelling all this magic always gives me an appetite. Are you hungry, dear?' she asked her husband.

'No, mine little pinkie, just tired, very tired.'

The Inspector rose to his feet. 'I must have air,' he shouted.

'Two lumps in mine,' said the ex-corpse. He looked at Victor and his wife. 'Thank you so very much for doing whatever it was that you did. Thanks to you, I'm a new man. Well, at least I'm a new old man, or an old new man. No matter, the most important thing, as far as I'm concerned, is that I'm here and alive again, thanks to you two and, of course, the Sergeant.'

'Well, it's good to see you up and about,' the Sergeant said happily. 'But can't you remember what happened? You know, er, before you, er, died?'

'Oh yes,' replied Fred Garden, only too happy to be of assistance. 'I was walking past the police station when a figure stopped me and asked me if I knew the way to Zanozay and, before I could answer, his face came very close to mine and I did notice a strong smell of sulphur . . .'

'I like the smell of sulphur,' Victor said quietly to himself.

The ex-dead man carried on, 'A second after that, both his arms grabbed my shoulders. The next thing I felt was two sharp pinpricks at the base of my neck. Life then just seemed to ooze out of me. There was nothing I could do. As I slowly floated down to the ground, the last thing I remember seeing before I died, was this face with two very long teeth somehow growing over his bottom lip and deep black eyes that seemed to shine. There was blood on his chin. I remember thinking maybe he'd cut himself shaving, but now I realise that it was my blood.'

The old King and Queen were sitting on the bench, listening to the poor man and, although they were both very tired, they still listened.

The Sergeant asked the R.R.T.L. (recently returned to life), 'How do you feel now? Is your hearing any better?'

'No, I don't drink at all, thank you!'

The ex-Queen broke into their conversation. 'The man who asked you the way to Zanozay, I don't suppose you noticed, when you were falling down, which direction he walked off in?'

The R.R.T.L. shook his head and said, 'I was dead, wasn't I?'

'Yes, I suppose so,' said the disappointed ex-Queen.

The Chief Inspector returned after his lungs had been filled with air at the station door, unseen by anyone . . . except Vernon.

'Everything all right, Inspector?' asked the Sergeant.

'Really!' answered the Inspector. 'Then please give her my regards.'

He disappeared into his office.

*   *   *

'Katchem, Katchem-by-the-Throat,' the voice shouted outside the coach station.

Vernon heard the coach arrive in the distance and the voice announce its arrival. He remained patient. He waited for his parents to leave the police station so

55

that, if he wished, he could follow them home. Eventually he saw his mother and father emerge out of the station. He thought, 'How tired they look.' He looked hard at his father and noticed he wasn't as pale as a fit Vampire should be. He then looked at his mother. She was very pale. As a matter of fact she was so pale she looked supremely fit.

'But,' Vernon thought, 'That could just be makeup and, underneath that pale makeup, she may not be as pale as she looks.'

He felt no sympathy towards them as they walked down the police station steps, dragging their feet down to the street level. Neither of them had the strength left to fly home so, as it was quite a nice night, they decided to walk.

As they walked away from the station hand in

hand, like two young lovers, Vernon followed, keeping a discreet distance behind them, all the way to their cottage. He then flew back to Bloodstock Castle, working out his plan to rid Gotcha of all his enemies and anyone else who happened to get in his way.

CHAPTER 5

First you see me, then see me not.
What a funny name I've got.

'We are now in Katchem,' said the beautiful stewardess. 'We hope you have enjoyed your journey with us and that you will ride with us again. Please do not leave the coach until it has completely stopped. Passengers wishing to continue their journey will please make their way to the terminal via the red area. On behalf of our coachman, Captain Broomstick, we thank you. Please make sure you do not leave any of your personal belongings on the coach. Thank you and have a nice night.'

Prince Igon was the last to leave the coach, or so he thought. He had picked up his luggage and was slowly walking away when he heard a sound that made him turn round. In the darkness he thought he saw a

medium-sized carrying case making its way towards him a few inches above the ground. There didn't appear to be anyone carrying the case, just the case itself. He narrowed his eyes to look harder but he saw no-one.

'Coachlag,' he thought. 'That's it, I'm suffering from coachlag.' The case made its way past him. It stopped and put itself down on the ground. Then a voice about six feet above the case said, 'Excuse me, but could you tell me the way to the best hotel. I think it's called the Black Cat.'

'Bat,' Igon said. 'The Black Bat.' He pointed automatically towards the Black Bat Hotel. 'It's only a few minutes' walk,' he said to the area surrounding the case.

'Thank you,' a voice said above the case.

Igon watched as the case lifted itself off the ground and went forward to the said hotel. From a few feet above the case there came the sound of a popular tune of the day being whistled.

As the whistling receded into the distance, Igon made a decision to stop Vernon at his own game. The clock in the centre of the village chimed ten. He knew of one or two coffee houses close by that stayed open late to catch the trade from the last few stage coaches. He knew also that if he wanted any information, or the latest gossip, that was where he would find it. It didn't much matter which coffee house, as they both served up the same gossip.

*   *   *

Vernon had the same idea. He'd followed his parents to their home, unseen. He'd been back to the castle to check it out... unseen. He now needed information and to get that he had to meet people, without them knowing who he was. Disguise, that was the only way to avoid being recognised. And a coffee house was a good place to meet people and get information.

The disguise was going to be difficult. There was no-one walking about from whom he could steal anything like a suit or a moustache or a beard, yet if he was going into a well-lit area he would have to be completely unrecognisable. He moved furtively from shadow to shadow and shop entrance to shop entrance. One of the shops was a clothes shop. It was too dark to see inside, but he could just about make out some figures in the shop window itself – dummies.

Now according to Vernon's reckoning, dummies

wore clothes. All he had to do now was to take one of the dummies out of the window and find a hiding place to change from his Vampire evening dress suit into something else, a sports outfit maybe.

All this was going through his mind as he very deftly and with the minimum of effort forced open the locked door of the shop. He slowly crept into the shop window and carefully picked up one of the dummies, except it wasn't a dummy but one of the window dressers getting the window ready for the sales which started the next day. As he lifted the unfortunate window dresser off his feet, the man let out a scream that would have been heard the other side of Europe, if he hadn't fainted.

In the ensuing panic, Vernon, who was as much surprised as the window dresser, dropped him on the floor, picked up another dummy and ran as fast as his legs would carry him.

He hid behind a wall and took stock of his dummy. It was wearing a very pretty red dress with a very pretty red handbag and a very pretty pert red hat with a very pretty red feather. There was no time to put his own clothes on the dummy. All he could do was to climb into the dress, hat and red shoes to boot.

*   *   *

The male receptionist of the posh Black Bat Hotel was a rather nervous, twitching type of man, who wore a black suit. His face was the same colour as the moon. He didn't see the case enter the lobby of the hotel, having his back towards the main entrance at the time. He was busy sorting letters for the hotel guests and putting them in their pigeon holes.

'Excuse me,' a voice said, making the nervous man drop all the letters he was holding.

Without turning round he said, 'Whoops-a-buttercup! Now look what you've made me do!'

'I'm sorry,' the same voice said, as the man in black picked up the letters off the floor.

He turned his face towards what he thought was going to be a hotel guest. As he turned he smiled the set smile of all hotel receptionists.

'Now then, Sir, what can I ... do ... for ... you?' His voice faded away as he realized he was actually talking to nothing and looking at no-one. He twitched his shoulders, then his left eye, and said, 'Humff.' His trained eyes looked professionally round the hotel lobby and saw no-one. He turned back to the job of sorting the letters.

'Excuse me,' the voice said again. 'I'd like a room please.'

The receptionist almost jumped out of his black suit and quickly turned in the direction of the voice. He once again saw no-one. Putting his well-shaped and beautifully manicured hands on the reception desk, he leaned over it to look for the owner of the voice, thinking it might be some small person. He saw only a case resting on the floor in front of the desk. He leaned even further over to see if a very small person was hiding behind the stationary suitcase. He saw no-one.

A fat lady, some would even say a huge lady (one arm alone weighed over four stone and her legs were bigger than her arms), rolled slowly over to the reception desk and asked for her keys.

'Room 27,' she said sharply, feeling pangs of hunger, not having eaten for the last ten minutes. 'Hurry, you silly little man,' she commanded as three of her four chins wobbled to a halt.

A little to the left they both heard a voice say, 'I was here first!'

The fat lady looked to her left, but could see no-one. She thought the receptionist was playing a joke by throwing his voice, as in a Punch and Judy Show.

'Well,' she thought, 'seeing that my name is Judy, I'll punch him!' Which she did. Hard, fast and straight with unerring aim and perfectly on target.

Within three seconds of the punch being thrown, the left eye of the receptionist looked very different from the right one. For one thing it was closed, for another it was swollen, and for yet another it was altogether a different colour. A minute ago both his eyes had been one colour, a rather deep, languid blue. His right eye was still blue, but his left eye was black as well as blue, as well as green, as well as purple.

From slightly to her left the fat lady heard a chuckle of enjoyment. So once more she lashed out with the same unerring aim. Three seconds later both his eyes were the same colour – blue, black, green and purple.

The fat lady drew herself up to her full width and said, 'Young man, I haven't come to this hotel to be insulted.'

A little to her left she heard a voice say, 'Oh well, to which hotel do you usually go?'

The poor receptionist never knew much about the handbag that hit him, except that it was large and extremely heavy. While he was falling to the floor and the fat lady was waddling to her room, he thought he saw a quill pen writing in the register. Out of sheer

curiosity, he looked to see if a name had been added or if he had dreamt it. He saw a name that wasn't there before he had been clobbered: a Mr C Menott, Room six. He remembered thinking, 'Good Lord, that's Wilf the Werewolf's room,' as he hit the floor and passed out.

The case made its way up the stairs. It stopped outside Room Six. A knocking sound was heard. There was no answer from inside the room. Mr C Menott saw a waiter walking down the corridor. The waiter couldn't see him. He only saw the case outside Room Six.

Mr C Menott knocked hard on the door, at the same time shouting, 'Let me out! Please, someone, let me out!'

The waiter stopped by the door as he heard the call for help, seemingly coming from inside Room Six. Mr C Menott carried on shouting, although he was standing by the waiter who now had his ear to the door. The waiter quickly took out his pass key and opened the door to Room Six. As he did so, Mr C Menott followed, sliding the case into the room with his foot. The waiter stood in the middle of the room. There was no-one to be seen. With a shrug of his shoulders, he left the room, not bothering to look at the suitcase that was now inside. As he left, he stepped over the case and closed the door.

C Menott lifted up the suitcase with a smile, not that anyone would have known, and put it on the bed. He opened it and unpacked an invisible suit, shirt and a very nice bright red cravat. He opened the wardrobe and hung them up. Only Mr C Menott could see them. He went into the bathroom and had a nice hot bath with lots of splashing and lots of singing. So much singing that the people in Room Five started knocking on the wall. He had almost finished his bath when the maid came into the room to turn down the bed. She didn't notice the door to the bathroom was open and, had she walked into the bathroom, she wouldn't have seen Mr C Menott anyway.

He was sitting on the dressing table chair, drying his hair with a visible towel, as the maid stood up from turning down the bed and started to leave. She was closing the door when, as always, she looked around the room to see if things were in order. She looked at the waving towel by the dressing table and, quite naturally, thought that the bedroom window must have been left open and was blowing the towel about. She walked back to where the towel was drying his hair and snatched it out of his hand.

Mr C Menott was almost as surprised as she was when he snatched it back. He then dropped it on the floor and, as she bent down to pick it up, he moved it with his hand. She followed the towel for a few unthinking seconds before realizing that the towel was travelling alone and she was chasing it. She stood up and walked swiftly to the door without bothering to turn round. Her sole ambition was to leave the room as quickly as possible. Once more Mr C Menott smiled to himself. He sat on the bed waiting for the arrival of the man who had sent for him: Wilf the Werewolf.

*   *   *

As Vernon made his way to the coffee house he worked out his plan in his mind. One: to get into the castle without being seen. That should be easy. Two: to get his old lab back in working order. That could take a little time. Three: to get Igon, his brother, his mother and his father, and Wilf the Werewolf to the castle without their suspecting anything was wrong. That was the easy part. He would forge a letter from the idiot police Inspector, telling them to be at the old laboratory at a certain time, as he (the Inspector) had captured Vernon and wanted them to identify the body.

'Oh yes,' he thought, 'that will get them all in one room at the same time and then I can kill them all at once. Wonderful! I am a genius!'

*   *   *

Valeeta made Victor a strong cup of hot tomato juice to cheer him up and to get some strength back into his tired body.

*   *   *

Sergeant Salt saw to it that Mr Fred Garden was taken safely home and, under Section Four of the Fifth Section of the Third Declaration, he was made to sign the Secrecy Note 222A, which confirmed a strict promise never to tell anyone that he had signed the Secrecy Note 222A, or that he had once died and had been brought back to life.

*   *   *

Inspector Speekup tried to regain control of himself by exercising in his office and shouting, 'Come in,' even though nobody knocked.

*   *   *

Mr C Menott was lying unseen and unheard on Wilf's bed when he heard a knock on the door.

'Come in,' he shouted to the door.

Mr C Menott saw the nervous receptionist and the manager of the Black Bat Hotel almost slide into the room. Mr C Menott stayed as still as possible and ignored the manager's first, second and third 'ehrem'.

'Maybe he's having a bath, Sir?' the nervous receptionist said, looking slowly around the room through the two swollen slits that were now his eyes.

'Knock on the bathroom door and find out,' barked the grumpy manager. It was, or should have been, obvious to the manager that the eyes of the receptionist were in need of medical care. But that was ignored.

'Hurry, man,' shouted the manager as he snapped his fingers in front of the poor receptionist's face. 'Can't you do a simple thing like knock on a door?'

'If I could see the door I might, Sir, but I'm finding it very difficult to see anything at the moment, Sir.'

'Oh dear,' said the pompous manager. 'Oh very dear. Why I ask, why do I have to have people like you working for me, eh? You and your kind are nothing but problems.' The manager breathed heavily. 'How many fingers am I holding up, eh? Come on, man, how many fingers, eh?' The manager held up four of his fingers in front of the almost sightless receptionist who was now twitching his shoulder rapidly. 'Stop that, stop that twitching at once. How many fingers am I holding?'

'Sir, I can't even see your hand, let alone your fingers.'

'Oh dear me. Oh very dear me. Leave me, go downstairs and bathe your eyes, you twitching oaf. Get out of my sight. Do you hear?

'Three,' said the receptionist tentatively.

'What?'

'Three fingers, Sir.'

'No.'

'Nine?'

'Get out, get out of this room, you're guessing.'

The receptionist bowed and almost curtsied as he turned to leave the room. It took him a full minute to find the door. He walked into the wall twice. The manager snorted and swaggered to the bathroom door, one hand bunched into a fist ready for a hard knock.

Having watched all that had been going on, Mr C

Menott, still lying on the bed thought, 'I don't think I like you, Mr Manager. I think you should be taught a short, sharp lesson.'

He rose from his bed and made his way towards the door leading to the corridor. He waited until the manager realized that there was no-one in the bathroom and came back to the door where Mr C Menott was waiting. The manager opened the door and left the room, very closely followed by the unseen Mr C Menott.

Once in the corridor the manager bowed and scraped to the hotel guests as they made their way to and from their rooms. It was then that Mr C Menott grabbed the seat of the manager's trousers with one hand and his jacket collar with the other and ran with him along the corridor. No-one in the corridor could see Mr C Menott. What they saw was the manager running with the collar of his jacket almost over his head and the seat of his trousers all bunched up at the back, while his eyes were almost hanging on his cheeks with disbelief.

He was pushed all the way down to the lobby of the hotel where a queue was beginning to form outside the restaurant door. They all looked at the manager making a fool of himself. Odd words were heard from the people in the queue. Words like 'drunk' and 'shameful' or 'shamefully drunk'.

Mr C Menott put his face as close as he could to the manager and shouted, 'Yes, I'm very drunk. But not too drunk to tell you not to eat in that restaurant.'

Mr C Menott lifted the manager's right arm and pointed it towards the door of the restaurant. He also moved the manager's lower jaw as he shouted, 'Any-

one who stays here is a fool.' He then jigged around the foyer again.

Within an hour the receptionist had been moved from the reception desk to an office with 'Manager' written on the door. He had also been given a very pretty secretary, although at the moment he couldn't see her as she carefully bathed his eyes. The old manager was thrown out of the hotel and was never allowed back in again.

CHAPTER 6

Wilf the Werewolf has a strange habit.
He turns into a turkey, a duck or a rabbit.

Vernon and Igon made their separate ways to the latest and most modern coffee house in Katchem, called The Sip and Dip. Both the coffee and the food were good, a sure fire reason for success. Their speciality was the coffee, it was always hot, strong and sweet. The biscuits served with it (free) were made in a special way. They were long, thin and one end turned to the left or right for holding, so that it was impossible to accidently dip your finger in the hot coffee if you wanted to dunk your biscuit.

Igon arrived a few minutes before Vernon. He looked at the long queue, but he was quickly seen by the head waiter, Nick-the-Greek (why they called him Nick-the-Greek, no-one knew, as he was an

Italian called Guiseppe). Before you could say 'Ga-
ciamo Robinsonio' Nick-the-Greek clicked his thumb
and forefinger together and as if by magic a table
with two place settings was found.

'Followa mea pleasea,' Nick-the-Greek said, with
a heavy Gotcharian Italian accent. There was an
angry murmuring from the queue as Igon was ush-
ered to the table. But that was soon stopped by the
quick flash of Nick-the-Greek's dark eyes.

'Silenceo, havea youa noa idea whoa thisa isa?' He
pointed a long finger towards Igon. The long queue
shuffled their feet and looked down. They knew that
if they wanted a table they had to be quiet. Igon
followed Nick-the-Greek with an embarrassed smile
as he flicked people out of their way with a long table
napkin.

'You shouldn't have gone to all this trouble, Nick,'
Igon said.

'Itsa noa troublea,' Nick grinned. 'Itsa noa troublea ata all.'

Igon sat down as Nick flicked the long table napkin
with unerring aim towards the back of the neck of a
young waiter, stinging him smartly. The sharp pain
made the waiter spin round, ready to shout at the
person who had caused it, but when he saw who it
was, he forced a grin and began to push customers to
one side. Nick looked at the waiter and hissed:

'Look aftera hima, si.' The young waiter nodded
his head, proud to have been noticed by Nick-the-
Greek, but not too proud to rub the inflamed area at
the back of his neck.

'What would sir like?' he asked Igon, showing him
a spotlessly clean menu coupled with a bright smile.

Igon took the menu but only glanced at it.

'Just a coffee please,' he whispered. The young waiter smiled, bowed and left.

Vernon arrived at the back of the queue dressed in the dress, hat, handbag and shoes he had stolen from Asquit Qutems in the High Street. He was having a great deal of difficulty walking in the shoes. The soles of them were at that moment facing each other. In the red shoes and the red dress, he looked like a bow-legged pillar box.

Nick-the-Greek with his great experience knew that, looking like she did, this woman could cause him trouble and a lot of embarrassment if she wasn't taken care of right away.

With no hesitation, he flicked his thumb and fore-finger and his napkin at the same time (a great gift) and shouted over the heads of the subdued queue.

'Senorita, senorita, pleasea comea thisa way.' Vernon wasn't yet used to being a woman and looked round to see who this idiot was shouting at. Nick-the-Greek tried again.

'Hey, senorita, thisa waya pleasea ... hey, senorita ... youa ina the reda dressa ... youa lookinga ar-ounda everya timea Ia saya youa ina thea reda dressa.' Vernon still looked round. Nick was now getting excited.

'Hey, youa, thea onea who looka uglya and stupido ... youa, wassa matta witha youa?' Nick realised that his shouting was getting nowhere, so he flicked out his napkin straight at Vernon's bare arm. The sudden sting enraged Vernon.

'What do you think you are doing, you great fool?' he shouted.

Nick-the-Greek turned away, knowing that she couldn't be talking to him like that; no-one talked to him like that except his mother-in-law. While Vernon pushed his way through the queue to this madman who had just hurt him, Nick-the-Greek turned round just in time to see this crazed woman with an arm raised ready to strike him. He ducked the blow saying, 'Thisa waya Ladya, youa surea causea a lota troublea, si?'

Vernon followed Nick-the-Greek, not because he wanted to, but because the impetus of the blow he was delivering carried him on and ever on. The blow landed on the table where Igon was sitting. It split his table in two.

'Hello,' Igon said politely. Vernon gathered his calm, smiled with great difficulty and tried to say he was sorry but he found it hard as he had never said he was sorry to anyone before. Igon pooh poohed the idea of an apology and asked Nick-the-Greek if he could have another table and if maybe the lady could join him. Vernon nodded and Igon smiled, neither of them knowing who the other one was.

Igon looked at Vernon, thinking she was a most attractive woman, although he thought a couple of her teeth were a bit too big. Vernon looked at Igon and thought it odd that he had never seen such a striking man before. He must be new to the area and wasn't around before he, Vernon, was statued. Igon spoke first.

'May I ask your name, Madamoiselle?'

'Vernon,' Vernon answered, noticing a strange look on Igon's face.

'Pardon?'

'Vernon,' Vernon answered again. 'Valerie Vernon'.

'May I call you Val, or do you prefer Miss Vernon?' Igon asked shyly.

'Er yes,' answered Vernon.

'Then it shall be Val,' Igon said with great aplomb. 'And you must call me I . . .' But before he could finish what he was about to say, the young waiter came with the coffee. Vernon looked at Igon.

'Very well, I will call you I, and you will call me Val.' Igon asked Val if she would like something to drink before eating. The lady Vernon didn't think before answering, 'Yes please, a bloody mary with real blood.' He realised what he had said as soon as the words were out. Every nerve in his cold body became taut. He knew that he had made a mistake, but luckily for him all the people around thought he had made a joke. His nerve ends relaxed as everyone laughed. Someone at the next table shouted, 'Why not, and I'll have a chin and tonic.' The waiter smiled and walked away.

'Are you married, Val?' asked Igon. Vernon took at least five seconds to remember that he was Val, and said 'No.'

'How come a beautiful girl like you isn't married?'

'Because I haven't been asked,' Vernon said curtly. Igon thought he'd better change the subject.

'What are you doing in Katchem, Val?'

'I'm looking for someone.'

'Maybe I know the person you're looking for, after all I've lived here all my life.'

'He's very ugly.'

Igon picked up his coffee cup and was just putting

it to his lips when he asked, 'What's his name?'

'Igon,' Vernon hissed. Igon's coffee not only went over Vernon but several other people.

'Igon?'

'Yes, why, do you know him? Can you tell me where he is? Where can I get in touch with him?'

'Igon?' Igon asked again.

'Yes, Igon.' Vernon was beginning to shout.

'Please keep your voice down, Madame,' Igon said quickly, his own voice shaking with nerves. 'Let me get a napkin and wipe the coffee off your dress ...'

'Forget the dress. I'm looking for Igon and you seem to know him. Now I want you to tell me where he is.' Vernon had Igon's hand in his but there was no affection in the grasp, just pure pain.

'You're hurting my hand, Valerie,' Igon whispered. Vernon looked down at their clasped hands and saw that the hand in his was beginning to turn blue. He let it go and watched as it twitched and pumped its way back to life.

Vernon tried to keep calm. 'I'm sorry, I,' he said with great difficulty. Igon tried to smile. There was no doubt that he had been shaken when he heard his name. He wondered what this beautiful woman would want with Igon, the old Igon. He took a gamble. He leaned over the table and, in a very low voice, he asked:

'Are you my Mumsy, the Mumsy that left many years ago?' There were tears in Igon's eyes. Vernon was now out of his depth and there was only one thing to do. Attack, hard and fast. He had found over the years that the best thing to do was hit out and run. He hit Igon and ran.

Igon sat on the floor with a busted lip swelling more every half second and through the water in his eyes he thought he saw the lovely Valerie in her pretty red dress run up the High Street, and in his befuddled mind he saw her take off from the ground and soar into the dark sky. He felt his sore lip with a tentative finger, wondering if she could have been Mumsy. She certainly hit hard enough to be his beloved Mums. If not, who was she? What did she say her name was? Valerie, Valerie Vernon ... Vernon ... He looked up at the sky through the coffee house window. Across the moon he saw a tiny figure flying towards Bloodstock Castle and he suddenly thought, Vernon! That attractive girl was Vernon. Thank Heavens Vernon hadn't known that he'd been talking to Igon. It gave Igon a slight advantage because Vernon obviously didn't know that Igon had been changed.

Igon left the coffee house after paying his bill, thinking all the time, 'I've got to get Vernon before he gets me.'

*　　*　　*

Vernon was inside the castle and, more than that, he was inside his old lab. A look of nostalgia came across his hard Vampirian face. So did a rather large spider, who was obviously annoyed at being disturbed after three years of living in perfect surroundings. Vernon gently lifted the large spider off his face and, with great care and almost affection, he gingerly put it on the floor and stood on it. As he did so, every spider's web in the lab seemed to go taut. It was as if all the spiders knew that the Master was back in their midst. Bats flew around his head and squeaked their welcome. Rats gathered at his feet as if in homage. As he walked, the crowd separated, leaving him a path to walk along.

A sleeping eagle, almost as big as Vernon, opened one eye and looked at him as he strolled around what the eagle had thought was his domain. The eagle thought he was the master here. It was the perfect place, with food a-plenty; rats, small birds, bats and a thousand different insects to eat when he felt like it. No other 'thing' was going to take over while he was here.

The eagle shook himself awake, letting all his feathers settle into their alloted positions. He watched as Vernon picked up old phials and bottles. The big bird then strutted and stretched on its perch in the darkness of the lab. It slowly lifted its wings into a twelve foot span. It rose majestically into the air. Then, as if on a laser beam, flew at such tremendous speed and power that small rocks fell from the roof of the underground lab.

Undeterred, Vernon looked at the giant bird flying straight at him. He spread his legs to give himself more balance. When the eagle was six feet away from him, he quickly raised his arm and pointed straight at the determined bird. The concentration in Vernon's eyes was something to behold.

The bird put its claws forward as if to tear the head from Vernon's shoulders. The claws were as big as those of a lion. Suddenly, with no more than four feet to go, every feather on the massive eagle fell off. The naked bird fell like a stone to the ground. It was killed instantly. The dead, naked bird was no further than a foot away from Vernon. Another foot behind the

dead eagle was a huge pile of eagle's feathers.

Bats and rats, birds and anything that was alive in that lab, all thought the same thing: the Master is back.

*　　　*　　　*

Wilf walked into the hotel room. He was now the manager of the Gotcha National Soccer Team and soon they would be playing the Gerts in their annual home international. Wilf the Werewolf was still a great attraction in Gotcha, not only because he was the National Team Manager, but because every full moon he really did turn into a Werewolf with a wolf's face and hair all over his body. At the moment Wilf was quite normal and would be for the next few days, as the full moon was still two nights off.

He threw his leather jerkin casually on the bed.

It came back to him through the air, just as casually, followed by a warm and friendly laugh. Wilf caught the jerkin and looked hard at the bed. He saw a human shape but not the human who was making it.

'Is that you?' he asked.

'Who else?' was the reply.

Wilf smiled and held out his hand to be shaken. He felt his arm being firmly shaken up and down.

'How are you?' Wilf asked.

'Fine, how about you?'

'I'm fine too,' Wilf said, 'Sit down.'

'I have.'

'Oh,' said Wilf. 'This is going to be difficult.'

'Not really. I'll stay here. I'm on the edge of the bed.'

'Good.' Wilf moved and sat in the chair next to the edge of the bed.

'Right, Wilf. Why have you sent for me? All those first class fares and twenty rems for expenses. That's a lot of money, Wilf, just for a friendly chat ... who do you want put out of action?'

'Well, it's not really like that, C.M. Although it's close. You know that I'm the manager of the Gotcha Soccer Team? Well, we play Gertcha in a home international in a couple of week's time, so I was wondering, er, if you would like to see the game ..?'

Mr C. waited for Wilf to continue, but Wilf had stopped.

'See the game?' asked the perplexed man. 'Sure,

I'd like to see the game. I'm as keen on football as you are. Would I be sitting with you on the bench?'

'Well, er, not exactly.'

'Well, where would I see the game from?'

'From the pitch itself,' Wilf answered in a quiet voice.

'I'm not with you.'

'That's right. You'll be with the team, my team, out there, on the field. And what I'd like you to do is, er, just to make it a bit more difficult for the Gerts to get the ball. You know, a little trip here, and a little trip there. That is, when none of my men is anywhere near the fella you'll be tripping. Because we don't want the referee giving fouls against us. Fouls that you'll be committing...'

'Isn't that cheating?'

'I would think so, yes.'

There was a pause before Mr C. spoke again.

'What's in it for me?'

'Twenty-five krooms. In cash.'

'Thirty?'

'Shake.' Wilf's hand was pumped up and down again.

'I'm surprised at you, Wilf. I've never put you down as a cheat.'

Wilf thought that it was time he changed the subject and did so by asking, 'How's your mum?'

'Oh she's fine, how's yours?'

'She's fine as well. She still gets a little upset when I change into a Werewolf, but she's become quite used to it now. Although I'm starting to get a few problems.'

'What kind of problems?' asked Mr C. from

another part of the room.

'Well, last November when it was full moon, I didn't turn into a Werewolf. I, er, changed into a turkey.' Wilf looked a little embarrassed.

'A turkey?' The question came from yet another part of the room.

'Yes,' Wilf said, looking towards the wardrobe. 'You see, on the night of the full moon I start to see the wolf hair growing on my hands.' He showed the wardrobe the back of his hands. 'It's very soft hair. Lots of people think wolves' hair would be thick and rough but it's quite soft really. When I see the hair on the back of my hands I know that I'm turning. So I tell Mum that I'm wolfing again and she says, "Off you go, love," and I go into the forest. Only last November, I didn't see any hairs, just feathers, small ones at first and then bigger ones. Well, within an hour, I was a full-sized turkey. A very big turkey. One of the biggest I've ever seen. Have you seen a seven foot turkey?' Wilf asked.

Before Mr C. could answer, Wilf carried on, 'Naturally I didn't tell Mum, I just shouted through the door that I was wolfing again, 'cos I didn't want to upset her.'

'Of course not,' the voice came from under the bed.

'Anyway, I went out and the next day I was captured by three farmers and they put me in a pen. I could tell by their conversation that they intended to fatten me up for Christmas and either sell me or eat me themselves. Well, I was a bit lucky that night because I just turned back into a Werewolf and they recognized me as Wilf and they let me go. But I'm sure they thought I'd eaten the turkey.'

'It all sounds very strange,' the voice said from behind the curtain.

'I think it's being caused by stress.'

'You think so?' the voice spoke from inside the wardrobe.

'Yes, the stress of being a football manager. Last month, I turned into an enormous rabbit and it was Easter so I had to stay hidden till I changed back into a Werewolf again. There's no fun it it anymore.' Wilf stopped speaking and looked very sad and depressed.

They both remained silent for a few moments, then Wilf said, 'How long is it now since your mum's seen you?'

'Almost twelve years. Although I've seen her, she hasn't seen me. My dad tells everybody I've left home. All our friends think my mum's potty. They think she's started talking to herself. But she's really talking to me. I've been like this now for nearly thirteen years.'

'Has it been that long?' Wilf asked.

'Yes, thirteen years. Mind you, I've had a lot of fun being invisible but it's got lots of drawbacks, like girls. It's a bit awkward trying to date a girl, telling her you'll meet her at six o'clock under the lamp and she's there, but she's not sure you are.'

'That's true. It's the same for me. I mean to say, if I've made a date with a girl and it's a misty night and I've changed into a Werewolf, well, she sees me walking towards her and she thinks I've bought her a fur coat.'

They fell silent again, each with his own thoughts, each feeling sorry for one another, but mostly for himself. Wilf was the first to break the silence.

'How did you become invisible?' he asked the empty chair.

'It was an accident,' the voice answered from the top of the wardrobe. 'I was thirteen and I picked up a bottle with no label on it. Like a fool, I opened it and, even more foolishly, I drank from it. It was a bottle of invisible ink and I haven't been seen since. I'll tell you something, Wilf, I'd never do a silly thing like that again.'

There was a great deal of sadness in Mr C Menott's voice, even though it was coming from the chimney.

*　　*　　*

Police Inspector Speekup was sitting in his office, having no idea how to combat Vernon. Vernon, on the other hand, had made a small explosive device

86

and placed it outside the window of the Inspector's office. At 2.15 a.m. the device went off with a tremendous bang. The Inspector looked up and said, 'Come in.'

*   *   *

Igon sat with the President and his wife, all three of them looking at *The Nightly Express* with the latest news.

*   *   *

Victor and Valeeta sat in their cottage. Valeeta was wondering how she could get in touch with her little boy, Vernon, while Victor wondered how their little boy, Vernon, would get in touch with them.

*   *   *

Wilf the Werewolf and Mr C Menott talked of old times and old games.

*   *   *

Vernon had stayed awake for as long as he dared into the morning, clearing the lab and getting it ready for the work he had to do. The sun was almost up when he wearily climbed into his old unmade coffin.

He snuggled down to sleep the sleep of the undead and, for the first time since he was a little boy, put his thumb in his mouth. He also said his prayers to the Great Drac, drifting into the Draculars he used to say as a little boy.

> '*In my coffin as I dream,*
> *Make Count Dracula hear my scream.*

Drac protect me all the time,
And keep me safe till evening chimes.
Drac bless Mummy and Daddy,
Granny Vicious and great Uncle Vigour.
Also Drac bless my pet rats,
Volcano, Vile and Vermin.'

CHAPTER 7

Down in a cold, dark and dank cave
Vernon's enemies are prepared for their grave.

Igon, Wilf, Victor and Valeeta all received their letters round about the same time. Each letter was the
same, clear and to the point:

> Dear . . .
>
> We have discovered a body, which we believe
> to be that of Vernon the Vampire. It is a dead
> body with a stake through the heart. We are
> holding the said body in the vaults of Blood-
> stock Castle and would like you to come there
> at two minutes before midnight tonight to help
> us in the identification of the said body.
> The main castle gates will be open. This letter
> must be kept secret.

The letter was signed by Chief Inspector Speekup. They had all read their letters and each of them had kept it a secret from the others. Victor and Valeeta were the most upset and Valeeta was not looking forward to identifying the body of her son.

The ex-King and Queen were the first to arrive. As the letter had said, the main gates were open and both Victor and Valeeta knew their way about the castle better than anyone. After all, they had lived and ruled from there for over a hundred years. Once inside the castle, they both stood inside the great hall which was dimly lit by rush torches placed in brackets on the wall. The torches threw out a flickering light which consistently shadowed then cleared. They gazed around the hall; it looked and felt huge.

'I never realized how cold it was when we used to live here,' the ex-Queen said.

'Ya,' was Victor's reply.

They walked proudly towards the door, well over fifty feet away, which would lead them down into the vault, over three hundred feet below the castle. The echo of their footsteps bounced off the five-foot-thick walls, the click of Valeeta's sharp heels mixing with the slap of Victor's boots. Valeeta, apart from being depressed at having to identify her son's body, was also feeling the cold. She sneezed. Just a gentle, feminine sneeze. But the hall was so large and so high that it took two minutes before the echo of that sneeze died away.

When they had almost reached the vault door the ex-Queen said, 'You would think that someone would look after this place, at least have it dusted now and again. It was never like this when we lived here. Everything shone when we lived here. Why when we lived ...'

'Shut up, mine dear,' Victor said, with enough command in his voice to make her do so. He blew the dust away from the sign hanging on the door. It seemed that only the dust had kept the sign in place. For, as the dust moved, the sign fell to the floor. The crash echoed round the hall just as the echoes of Valeeta's sneeze were fading away.

Victor ignored the sign on the floor and carefully opened the creaking door. He knew it was the right one. He led the way down the winding steps to the vault below. He held Valeeta's hand as they made their way into the damp darkness, guided only by a distant light. The door closed of its own accord.

* * *

Igon read and re-read the letter which he had found on the floor behind his door. He tore at the seal without looking at it. He called for his horse and made his way to the castle, wondering why the Inspector had asked him to identify the body of Vernon. He wondered, but never questioned.

He tied the horse to a hitching rail and looked around him. He seemed to be the only one there, although he had thought that someone else might have been asked to identify the body as well as himself. He made his way to the old iron gates that were to be open. He didn't know whether he was relieved or not when he found them so. This was not going to bring back pleasant memories for him, as he had lived in the castle for nearly all his life as one of the ugliest men who had ever been seen, not only in the castle, but anywhere.

He went through the open gates and into the courtyard, hoping that it was Vernon who had been found. If it was, it would mean that many people would be able to live their lives without the constant fear that Vernon would eventually find them and kill them.

As he entered the great hall, a flood of unhappy memories seemed to take over. Ugly memories, sad memories. He tried to think of one happy moment he had spent as a child in this forsaken castle, but sadly he couldn't. The only person who had treated him with any kindness whatsoever had been Valentine. Never once had he been unkind to him. But in those days he had only ever seen Valentine once every three or four weeks.

Igon made his way to the door that led to the vaults below, the vaults he knew so well from the old days. But now he walked to the door majestically – one of the most handsome men in the world, slim and erect in a white uniform that looked as if it had been painted on him, it fitted so well. The echo of his steps followed him in perfect rhythm.

He reached the door and picked up the dusty sign from the floor, thinking, 'In the old days I was hit on the head a few times with this.' He pulled the door open and heard the familiar creak as he made his way down the stairs.

*   *   *

Valentine looked at the letter he had just been handed. He thanked the servant with a nod. The servant bowed and left the room. Valentine read the letter with great relief. Vernon was dead and also, according to the letter, he was skewed. That meant he was dead forever. That meant he couldn't harm anyone again.

Valentine thought, 'That Inspector Speekup must be much cleverer than I thought. Although I'm not looking forward to this, I must go. Then, when I've seen Vernon, I can tell the people that they can once more live happily and in peace, live without fear or terror. I must think of the people, the people who have given me a great responsibility, although it's hard not to think of Victor and Valeeta at a time like this. However, I'll not tell them until I'm sure it's Vernon.'

The hardest part of the whole journey for Valentine would be to get past his own guards without their knowing that he was going out to the castle. He knew that there would be at least three armed guards outside the very room he was now in and three more guards on each floor.

He picked up his top hat and went to the door. He opened the door and walked out slowly backwards, with the top hat held almost over his face, while at the same time bowing as he moved backwards saying, 'Thank you, Mr President. You're very kind, Mr President. Yes, Mr President. And please, Sir, give your lovely wife my very best regards . . .'

The three guards ignored the man leaving the President's office. They would have been more interested in someone who was going in, rather than coming out.

Once outside, he kept as close as he could to the shadows. He went to the stables, harnessed one of the horses to a small buggy and drove elegantly out of the presidential grounds without once being stopped.

He arrived at the castle gates, which the note had said would be open. He stopped the horse and buggy outside the gates and walked through, leaving the horse tied, but free to reach the grass on the edge of the patch leading to the big castle doors. He crunched his way to the massive doors and found them open.

Inside the great hall of the castle he felt strange, as if he had never left the place and, at the same time, as if he had never been there before. It was very strange and quite unnerving. The light from the torches hanging from the walls was now low, making the shadows deeper.

He walked along the chess-patterned floor to the door leading down to the vaults. It all felt different from when he was a child and used to run wild in the great hall. He had never seemed to hear the echo of his footsteps then.

As he reached the door he thought once more, 'I do hope it is Vernon.' He opened the door and, at the same time, kicked away the sign with his foot, allowing the door to open freely.

* * *

Wilf actually saw his letter come under the door of his hotel room. He looked at it and, at first, wondered what it was. The thought of opening the door to see who had delivered it, never even entered his head. He picked up the sealed letter and turned it over, first looking at the seal. It was then that he thought of opening the door, but the corridor was completely empty. He walked back into his room, snapped the sealing wax and read the letter. Afterwards, a large grin covered his face.

'Great news,' he said aloud.

'What?' Mr C Menott said from an open drawer.

'Vernon's dead. At least, that's what the Inspector thinks and they want me to go and identify the body.'

'And will you?'

'It will be a pleasure.'

'He's not very popular then?'

'Poison's more popular.' Wilf made his way to the door. As he reached it, he turned and said to the room in general, 'I'll see you later then. OK?'

'Fine,' said the voice next to him. Wilf didn't see the smile on Mr C Menott's face.

As Wilf walked across the foyer of the hotel to the main exit door, a porter asked him if he was going to beat the Gerts that year.

'If everything goes to plan, yes.' He smiled at the porter just before he tripped up over nothing.

The porter rushed to help Wilf to his feet.

'Are you all right, Sir?'

'Yes, I'm fine, thank you. I wonder what I tripped over?' Wilf looked down and saw nothing on the ground.

'Can I call you a hansom cab?' the porter asked.

'Just call me a cab, I already know I'm handsome.'

The porter laughed and went outside to whistle a cab.

Wilf gave the address to the driver; 'Bloodstock Castle'. The driver's eyes widened as he flicked his whip in the direction of the horse's rump.

Alone in the cab, Wilf read the letter again in the reflection of the cab light until he arrived at the castle.

After he had paid the driver Wilf saw a horse with a buggy attached to it and thought, 'That will be Inspector Speekup's carriage. Good, he'll be able to give me a lift home.'

Once inside the castle, he looked up at the roof of the hall. It was almost as big as a cathedral. He stopped for a moment and listened to the spluttering torches. One or two of them had already gone out. Wilf hoped they would be replaced by the time he and the Inspector left. He looked around the great hall and, out of devilment, clapped his hands together once. Seven perfect echoes came back, followed by seven less perfect echoes, then seven more, until silence once more took over.

He walked as silently as possible to the door leading to the vaults. As he reached the door, he picked up a sign lying on the floor and shouted, 'Shall I throw it?' The words came back: THROW IT, THROW IT ... THROW IT, THROW it, throwit throwit ... throwit, rowit, witwitittt ... Wilf looked up, shook his head and put the sign silently back on the floor.

He opened the vault door and stood on the threshold. As he looked round again, he clapped his hands very loudly several times. He then went behind the vault door and kept coming back into the great hall saying, 'Thank you, thank you very much, ladies and gentlemen, you're so kind,' to an unseen clapping audience. As he closed the door for the last time he heard: 'So kind, so kind, so kind, so kind ... ind ... ind ... ind ...'

*   *   *

The streets of Katchem were empty of any form of movement, human or otherwise. The whole village was dead and covered in thick darkness.

The Inspector replaced his office curtain. He had no idea of how to capture Vernon. His only hope was that Vernon would turn into a nice man and go away. But he knew that would never happen.

He sat once more behind his desk. He lifted his papers and straightened them, putting them back into the exact position they were in before he had picked them up. Nervously, he walked over to the curtains and peered out into darkness as black as the inside of a tomb. He dropped the curtains and almost ran back to sit at his desk. He looked at his fingernails. They had almost disappeared.

He quickly opened the small drawer of his desk and took out a flat bottle. Without bothering to use a glass, he drank from the bottle itself – half of it in one go. He put the cork back and held it close to his trembling body with shaking hands. He was bravely trying not to drink any more but he couldn't stop himself. He pulled the cork from the bottle with his teeth, spat it across the room and finished off the rest of the bottle in one greedy gulp.

He dropped the empty bottle into the wastepaper basket by his desk. It was the third bottle of Doctor Strong's Nerve Tonic that he had put away that evening. He knew he was hooked and that the continual drinking was doing him no good.

Sergeant Salt sat at his desk, drinking a cup of hot

sweet tea from an old tin cup. The swing door of the police station burst open, nearly making him spill the tea all over his uniform. As he controlled the cup, and himself, he looked at the still swinging door. A very vicious-looking dog, with the hairs on its back raised, and near-red eyes, slunk towards the Sergeant's desk. In its mouth the dog held a letter, a sealed one. It watched the Sergeant, letting the letter drop to the floor.

'Hello boy,' the Sergeant whispered nervously.

In reply the dog showed its long, yellow teeth, snarling softly as saliva continuously dropped from its wolf-shaped mouth. It looked completely wild.

It backed towards the swing door, never taking its eyes away from Sergeant Salt. He, by now, had one hand under his desk, wrapped round a piece of lead piping that was always hanging there for emergencies such as this, while the other hand took a lump of meat out of his half-eaten sandwich and, as casually as possible, tried to throw it to the dog.

It was a good throw and the meat landed within a good sniff of the dog's wet nose. Its bright burning eyes never left the Sergeant, and never once looked at the meat, as it backed out of the police station. The Sergeant waited a full minute before letting his grip on the lead pipe relax.

He realized that the dog was somehow controlled to deliver that letter. Carefully he came round from his desk, never once taking his unblinking eyes off the swing door. He slowly bent down over the letter and, with one hand, felt for it on the floor. He rose and wiped the wet parchment on his thick, blue uniform pants. He took it to the nearest candle, holding it up

100

to the light to read. It was addressed to the Chief Inspector. He looked at the office door where he knew that the said Inspector was inside, drinking bottle after bottle of Doctor Strong's Nerve Tonic.

He thought, 'That nerve tonic must be working. After every bottle he gets more nervous.'

He walked into the Inspector's office without knocking. He knew that he didn't have time to waste, waiting for the Inspector to hear him knock and shout, 'Come in.' Without words, he gave the Inspector the letter.

The Great Detective or, as he was known by his men, the Defective Detective, held the letter in a shaking hand. He tore it open. He couldn't read it as his hands were shaking so much. Sergeant Salt moved round to the side of the desk where the Inspector was sitting, accidentally knocking over the wastepaper basket and seeing three empty bottles of Doctor Strong's Nerve Tonic rattle to the floor.

The Sergeant, being a tolerant man, ignored the bottles and gently but firmly held the shaking hand as the Inspector read out the contents of the letter:

My Dear Inspector,
You win. I am afraid that I cannot compete with such an agile brain as yours. The way you have distributed your meagre forces is brilliant, quite brilliant. A man of such immense skill can only be admired and so, Sir, I would like to do the honourable thing and give myself up to you personally, and to you alone, in the castle vaults tomorrow at dusk. No-one else must be with you. The shame of

giving in while some other person is present would be too much for me to take. I hope you understand as I'm sure you will, being the brilliant adversary you are, and a gentleman.

Yours, with great admiration,
Vernon.

The Inspector had stopped shaking about halfway through the letter. At that moment he was allowing a smile to turn into a grin and a grin to explode into a laugh. He looked at the nonplussed Sergeant who was now reading the letter himself.

'Well, Salt, he has met his match and knows it, eh, what?' the great detective crowed.

'I don't trust him, Sir,' the Sergeant shouted at the top of his voice.

'About one o'clock,' the Inspector answered back.

The Sergeant knew that there was no way he would be able to get through to his superior, although he smelt some sort of trap. To tell the Inspector that a mad dog had brought the letter, would have only evoked the answer, 'Two lumps in mine', so he decided not to tell him about the dog, or that he thought the letter was part of a trap.

The Inspector dismissed the Sergeant with a curt wave of his now-steady hand. He felt on top of the world as he re-read the letter, especially the sections 'cannot compete with such an agile brain' and 'a man of such skill'. He folded the letter up, put it in his pocket, then leaned back on his chair, put his feet on top of his desk and gently rocked back and forth, rehearsing the words: 'You are under arrest.'

Vernon would have been thrilled to have seen the

reaction the letter had received, as he knew it would do. A vain man, like the Inspector, would believe all the flattery you could pour on him and he would be there alone to make the arrest. But Vernon would not be there. Vernon knew he would be many miles away as the Inspector walked into the laboratory and found Igon, Valentine, Victor, Valeeta and Wilf the Were-wolf all dead . . .

CHAPTER 8

Vernon is dead – a stake through his heart!
But is Vernon dead? Or just playing a part?

Victor tried the door and it opened. He and Valeeta entered a small room that seemed to have been hewn out of rock. As they looked around the room they noticed another door in the opposite wall. Victor walked over and tried to open it. It was locked. He stepped back and looked around the door. A piece of parchment was sticking out, resting on the top hinge. Victor took it down and read it:

Will you please wait until the door opens automatically. It was signed by Inspector Speekup.

He showed the letter to Valeeta who nodded, saying, 'Well, there's very little we can do but wait, is there?'

'True, mine little dandelion, very true.'

They both looked about for a place to sit down and wait. Sitting close together on a piece of jutting rock, Victor folded his hands over his stomach. He heard a few 'tut tuts' as she watched him.

'Victor, aren't you ashamed?'

'Of vot, mine little elderberry?'

'Of being so fat that you can't fold your arms over your stomach. We've only been in here two minutes and I guarantee that you've put on three more pounds.'

Victor looked down to the much talked about offending part. 'I tink dere is sometink wronk wit me, mine little mushroom.'

'Yes there is. You're too fat, that's what's wrong with you.'

He looked up at her and nodded and smiled the

cheeky little smile that had first attracted her to him. She picked up Victor's hands and held them in her own, warming and squeezing them.

'Oh Victor,' she sighed. 'I hope it isn't Vernon whom the Inspector has found. But, I think that it must be. I mean to say, who else but a Vampire would have a stake through his heart? Surely we would have heard something about another Vampire in our district. Who can it be if it isn't Vernon?'

'I'm not knowink, mine little sweetpea.' Victor thought a little longer before saying, 'I saw Vilf the Verewolf the other night ant he never said anytink, ant he would be the first to hear anytink of that kind. He may be the last to buy a round but he's always the first vith the news.' Here he sighed heavily. 'Try not to vorry, mine little locust blossom.'

'Lotus,' the ex-Queen corrected.

'Ya, as I'm sayink, Lotust.'

They fell silent.

The door Victor and Valeeta had used to get into the small room opened and in came Valentine. The three of them looked at each other as if to say, 'What are you doing here?' After the surprise of seeing each other Victor took charge.

'Vot are you doink here?' he asked.

'Yes, what are you doing here? I thought this was to be a private affair?' The Queen seemed a little annoyed.

'So did I,' Valentine said. 'I received a letter from Chief Inspector Speekup asking me to come here and . . .'

Before he could finish the sentence, the outer door opened again and Igon came in. They all looked at

106

each other. Victor was the first to speak.

'Vot are you doink here?'

'I was telling you . . .' Valentine answered.

'No, not you, him,' Victor said, pointing to Igon.

'Yes,' said Valentine. 'What are you doing here?'

'I was told by a letter to come here and . . .'

Once more the door opened. This time, Wilf the Werewolf put his head around the door. Once more, everyone looked at each other as Victor took charge again.

'Vot are you doink here?'

Igon answered, 'I was just telling you . . .'

'Not you, him,' Victor snapped back.

'I told you, I had a letter . . .'

'No, not you, Igon,' Victor said sharply. 'Him.' He pointed to Wilf.

'Whom did you have a letter from?' asked the ex-Queen in her best royal calming-the-situation voice.

'Speekup,' said Wilf.

'All right, if it will help.' The old Queen shouted, 'Whom did you have a letter from?'

'Wait a minute,' Igon said. 'Don't you see, we all had a letter from Inspector Speekup. I don't want to broach a delicate subject, but I think we are all here for the same reason, to identify the, er . . .' He looked at Victor and Valeeta.

'That's right,' interrupted Valentine, also not wanting to hurt his mother and father's feelings any more than necessary.

Everyone nodded.

Wilf said, half aloud to himself, 'I hope it is him.'

The nodding continued – with the exception of Victor and Valeeta.

107

The room was so small that they all had to stand very close to one another. Eyes avoided eyes and conversations were kept at a trivial level. 'Haven't we had a wonderful summer?' was heard and 'Three krooms twenty? I said, no way, that's too expensive' followed by 'When we lived here the place was spotless.'

This kind of nervous conversation was kept going, partly out of respect for the mother and father of the body they were supposedly going to identify, and partly out of fear, the fear that none of them knew what was going to happen there, or when. They were all in one small room, trapped, each wondering why they had all had the same letter.

A new voice joined the conversation, a voice known to no-one in the room, except maybe Wilf. It said, 'Are those pearls you're wearing real, Mrs Vampire?'

Everyone's conversation stopped as each person looked at someone else, thinking that the other person had asked the rather impertinent question.

'Real? Real?' a rather astonished ex-Queen said. 'Of course they're real.' She looked in the direction where she thought the voice had come from.

'They must be worth a lot of krooms,' the voice said, this time from behind her, seemingly from where her husband was standing.

'Is that you talking, Victor?' the perplexed ex-Queen asked.

'No,' replied an equally perplexed ex-King.

Everyone, with the exception of Wilf, looked around the room at each other. Wilf thought he understood but, if he was right, he couldn't ask Mr C

Menott if he was there – he would look and sound silly.

Victor thought it was time he took over again, so he said to no-one in particular, 'Yes, whoever you are, they are real. I bought them for the Queen to celebrate our 75th anniversary, wedding, that is.' He looked at everyone in the room – well, everyone he could see. 'Isn't that true, mine little box of snuff?'

'Yes, my dearest,' the ex-Queen said with pride. 'I remember it as if it were only ten years ago. It was like this year, a leap year.' She nodded to the polite murmurings of congratulations.

Wilf stepped forward and, in a slightly agitated voice, asked if this year was a leap year.

'Ya,' said Victor as Valentine and Igon and Mr C Menott nodded. Victor continued like a school teacher, 'Thirty days hast September, April, June ant November. All the rest haff thirty-one, except for May alone . . .'

The old Queen thumped him hard on his back.

He continued, 'Except for July . . .'

Another thump landed on his back.

'Except for December alone, maybe?'

Another thump.

'February,' whispered his wife.

'Ya, February alone, vitch has dirthy-six . . .'

The thump on his back landed.

'Er, twenty days, er, tventy days . . . clear . . .'

Valeeta took over from the completely confused Victor. She spoke loudly and with precision, 'Which has twenty-eight days clear and twenty-nine in each leap year.'

She beamed, Victor nodded, Valentine seemed to have lost all interest and Igon applauded. Wilf was thinking, trying to work out when he would turn into a Werewolf or a turkey or anything and, according to his fingers, he was very close. A lot closer than he had thought, because he had forgotten that this was a leap year, which had put his calculations well and truly out of alignment.

He was holding his fingers up to count, when he noticed that the back of his hand was starting to swell and change colour. The main thought in Wilf's mind now was to get out of the room as quickly as possible before he changed into whatever it was he was going to change into. There was no guarantee that he would change into the old familiar Werewolf any more. The last time he had been a rabbit and he hadn't forgotten that he had been a turkey once.

He thought, 'If I do change into something other than a Werewolf, I hope it's something pretty. I've never been anything pretty.'

He made for the door to let himself out but it seemed to be locked. He put his almost-changed hand on the doorknob and pulled. The door stayed closed, very closed. Wilf felt at a loss. He didn't want to remain here while he changed. He liked to change in private. Even his own mother hadn't seen him change.

Once more he tried the door but it was still locked. He felt along the door hoping to find a secret lock, more in hope than anything else.

A quiet voice whispered in his left ear, 'It's no use, Wilf. The door is locked and your ear is now very furry.'

Wilf put his hand to the left ear and felt the fur.

'Is that you, Mr C?' an agitated Wilf asked.

'Of course it is.'

'Tell me what I'm turning into,' Wilf whispered once more.

'Something I've never seen before. I think they call them Kangaroos but, never having seen one, I'm not too sure.'

'Am I pretty?' Wilf asked out of the corner of his now pointed mouth.

'I wouldn't say that.'

'Oh. Well, will you stand in front of me, so the others can't see me changing?'

'Certainly, but it won't be of any help. I'm invisible.'

The others looked at Wilf and watched him change into something that none of them had ever seen before. To his credit, Wilf tried hard to be casual about the whole thing. But it's very difficult to be casual as your arms shrink, your ears grow and your legs become a completely different shape, not to mention the pouch that you are developing.

Wilf smiled a sad smile to his small audience as he sat on his huge tail. Valeeta was the first to come to her senses and she was also the first to speak.

'I think I'm going to be sick,' she said, as the little colour Vampires have drained completely away.

'Please, my little lettuce leaf, try ant get a hold of yourself,' Victor said as calmly as he could. 'Surely,' he continued, 'you have seen a giant gerbil before?'

'That thing is not a gerbil,' the ex-Queen said, pointing to a rather embarrassed kangaroo sitting on its

112

tail in the corner of the small room. 'What is it?' the ex-Queen almost screamed.

Igon said, 'I read a book once and I think they call them kangaroos. If I'm not mistaken, they're Australian,' he told the company brightly.

'Well,' the Queen said. 'If all Australians look like that, we should break off all diplomatic relations with them, as of now.' She looked straight at Valentine. Valentine kept his thoughts to himself.

Wilf said in a rather sad voice, 'I was hoping I would turn into something pretty.'

'You have,' the ex-Queen snapped. 'Something pretty awful.'

'Mrs Vampire, that wasn't nice, not nice at all,' a voice said from Victor's direction.

The ex-Queen, in fear and fury, wheeled round and hit Victor hard across the cheek.

A startled Victor said, 'Vot are you doink, mine little puff of pastry?'

Before anyone could answer, a large rock creaked open like a door. Everyone looked towards it. It opened on to blackness. No-one could see inside. Out of the blackness came a voice. A voice very similar to that of Chief Inspector Speekup.

'Ladies and gentlemen, and whatever Wilf is, will you please come into the laboratory. First ex-King Victor and ex-Queen Valeeta, then ten minutes later, please, Igon, then Valentine and last, but by no means least, whatever Wilf is. Thank you.'

'I'm a kangaroo,' Wilf said with a certain amount of pride.

'Are you?' said the voice. 'Well, whatever you are, Wilf, you will enter last. Is that understood?'

113

Victor and the ex-Queen composed themselves and majestically walked into the blackness. The door closed.

Once inside Vernon's old lab, the light began to get a little brighter and vision became reasonable. They walked forward to what looked like a coffin. It was on a table, ten yards away from them, with a candle at the head. Victor held on to his wife's shaking hand.

The ex-Queen, very proud and erect, suddenly took control of herself and slowly took her hand away from Victor. They looked at each other and gently held each other's throats with tender affection, smiled, then turned and made their way to the coffin

while the one candle flickered. The lid was off as they both looked inside. Lying there with a stake through his heart, was Vernon. He looked at peace.

The ex-Queen swayed a little as Victor held on to her. 'Oh my poor little boy, oh my dear, dear little boy. Why did this happen? Where did we go wrong?'

Victor blew his nose into his handkerchief, almost blowing the candle out.

'Who did this to you, my sweet little child? Tell your mummy who did this to you and I promise you, my boy, that I will avenge you.'

Victor put his arms around his wife's shoulders to try and gently take her away from the coffin. But she was strong and wasn't to be dragged away that easily.

She went into an old Vampirian death chant:

> Dracular, Dracular, Dracular Great,
> Look after my son who is now in this state.
> Keep him in peace in your arms, oh so good,
> And once every year touch his lips with your blood.

After one last look they turned away. As they turned, Vernon pressed down hard with his left foot at the bottom of the coffin. A net floated down, landing on top of a distraught Victor and Valeeta. As they tried to get out of the net, Vernon leaped out of the coffin, taking the false stake off by undoing the string holding it in place. His mother and father were now on the floor: a pathetic sight, as the two old people struggled to free themselves.

'Hello Mother, hello Father.'

Valeeta and Vernon stopped struggling and looked at Vernon. Both of them were confused.

Vernon laughed at them saying, 'Oh, this is good, this is. Oh yes, this is really good. Three years I've waited for this.'

'But I thought you were dead. We both did,' said Victor.

'You mean, you both hoped I was dead.' Vernon laughed a laugh that would have sent a chill down the back of the Great Drac himself.

'Why should we want you dead?' Victor asked from a sitting position. 'Your mother has been beside herself with worry about you.'

'That's true,' said the ex-Queen as she stirred to rise. 'You are still my little boy and we both love you so very much.'

'In a pig's eye you do,' Vernon's voice whipped out.

'Vere do you learn such language? Vere do you learn such bad talkink? How dare you talk like that to your mother.'

'Oh, shut up, you,' Vernon snarled. 'I'm the boss now. You're too weak to do any more magic and your flying is a joke. I'm going to kill you,' Vernon hissed, 'I'm going to kill you both. Then I'm going to kill Igon. But I'm going to kill him very slowly.' Vernon's dark eyes lit up with pleasure. 'Then I'm going to kill Valentine, either quickly or slowly, I haven't made up my mind yet. Then it's that stupid Wilf's turn. The next thing he's going to turn into is a corpse. Then I'll rule the Land of Gotcha and I'll rule with a rod of iron as in the old days before you were king and everything became soft.'

Vernon's mother and father were now both standing up in the net, dignity being out of the question.

116

Gradually the net was hoisted up to the roof, a matter of fifty feet, give or take an inch.

Vernon tied it up and shouted to them, 'If you as much as whisper when Igon comes in, I'll loosen the cord and you will drop fifty feet to the ground, give or take an inch. That, my lovely, sweet, caring parents will, I assure you, be very painful!'

He laughed as he watched them hanging in the net fifty feet above him, give or take an inch. He put the wooden stake back in place, as if it was stuck into his heart, and carefully climbed back into his coffin. He settled himself down to the one-breath-every-thirty-minutes routine. With his right foot, he opened the waiting-room door.

CHAPTER 9

Vernon says he has no love
for his Mum and Dad swinging above.

Wilf the Kangaroo was very busily trying to explain the new four-two-four formation which he had worked out to stop the Gerts from winning. He thought he heard a snigger of laughter from Mr C Menott as he tried to explain what he knew would be the soccer plan of the future and that, at the moment, he was working on a plan that didn't use wingers.

Igon looked into the darkness of the open door and asked, 'Where are the king and queen?'

A voice, similar to the Chief Inspector's, said, 'They have left by the back door.'

Igon went through the open door with a more than nervous look on his face. The door closed behind him.

'I'll tell you something, Mr President or Valentine.'

'You can call me Valentine, Wilf.'

'Thanks, Mr President. Well, I think there's something fishy going on in there and it wouldn't surprise me if that wasn't the last time we were to see Igon.' Wilf's kangaroo face nodded in the direction of the door Igon had just gone through.

'Oh come now, Wilf. You may be a kangaroo at the moment but you're not a fool. We have all heard the Inspector's voice and it's quite natural for the others to go out the back way. I mean to say, the Inspector wouldn't want us to be influenced in any way by meeting the others. He will want to hear what we all think separately.'

Wilf looked across to Valentine through his sad brown kangaroo eyes. 'Well, I don't know. I feel there's something wrong and we are here for a special reason.'

Wilf put his hand in his pouch and brought out an old crisp. He said, 'It looks as if the baby has been eating in bed.'

Mr C Menott laughed out loud.

Valentine looked at Wilf saying, 'Wilf, you know it's bad manners to laugh at your own jokes.'

*　　*　　*

Igon was almost at the side of the coffin. Vernon kept his eyes open, waiting for him. He hadn't seen him since the transformation. He lay there waiting, as still as death. As Igon looked down at Vernon both their memories came flooding back. Igon's was the pain he had had to suffer, while Vernon's was the joy of watching and causing Igon's pain. They looked at each other.

One thought to himself, 'I'm glad you're dead. You can't make anyone suffer again.'

The other one thought, 'I'm going to turn you back into that filthy, ugly animal you once were.'

Igon stayed by the coffin for as long as he thought it was decent to do so. He looked deep into Vernon's eyes and, for one millimetre of a second, he thought he saw the left eye give the tiniest flicker, but that was impossible . . .

'You are dead and I, for one, am glad. I'm only sad for the mother who loved you.'

As Igon turned to go, Vernon sprang up quickly and, from under the coffin's pillow, withdrew a syringe, already prepared with a potion that could put a man to sleep almost immediately.

'Igon,' he whispered. 'Don't go.'

Igon stopped in his tracks.

'Let us be friends, then I can go to the Great Drac with peace in my unhappy, broken heart. Give me your hand in friendship, old friend of mine.'

Igon turned slowly round and almost passed out as he saw Vernon sitting up in his coffin with a stake sticking out of his heart and his right hand outstretched in friendship. He automatically held out his own right hand. As the two hands met, Vernon gripped Igon's quickly and turned it palm up, while, with his left hand, he plunged the syringe into the exposed vein on Igon's wrist. Igon tried to pull away but Vernon was as fast as a cobra. The needle was in, then out, before Igon realized what was happening.

Vernon screamed with laughter as Igon swayed from the effect of the potion coursing through his veins. He jumped out of his coffin and looked up into the darkness. He could see the shadows of his mother and father.

'Look!' he shouted. 'Look, I've got Igon. I have him, he's mine. Look, you stupid fools.'

Vernon watched with the smile of a devil on his lips as he saw Igon become weaker and weaker.

His parents looked down and watched as Vernon guided a staggering Igon through a maze of shelves, phials, large bottles and bubbling crucibles towards the operating table. They watched Vernon lift a helpless Igon on to the table and fasten him with thick leather straps across his chest, then his wrists and ankles. Igon was secure and completely passed out.

Victor shouted down to his son, 'You are a fool, ant you vill never get avay vith this!'

'You are the fool, not me. You are the one who is going to die, not me. You are the one hanging from the roof. I'm here, so how can I be the fool?'

'Vernon, stop being a naughty boy and do as your daddy tells you,' his mother shouted.

'Never again will I do as my daddy tells me, never.'

He ran back to his coffin and climbed in, fastening the false stake to his left side and lying down.

He shouted, 'Now for the stupid Valentine!'

Vernon thumped the bottom of the coffin with his right foot. He heard the door open, then clearing his throat, he shouted in the voice of Inspector Speekup, 'Will you please come in, President Valentine.'

*   *   *

'Be careful,' Wilf said.

Valentine smiled at Wilf and walked into the dark lab. Wilf watched as he went through the doorway

121

and as the door closed once more, he sat on his tail.

'Are you there?' he asked.

'Here,' said Mr C. Menott.

'Where?' asked Wilf.

'In your pouch. I was getting cold, so I jumped into your pouch. There're no more crisps in here.'

'Come out,' ordered Wilf.

He waited a few seconds then asked, 'Are you out?'

'Yes. I'm sitting on your knee. It's more comfortable than sitting on the rocks or the floor.'

'I still think it's a trap and I'll tell you why.'

'Why?'

'Because I've been in there. That's Vernon's old lab and I've been in there and, as far as I can remember, there was no back door.'

'Are you sure?' asked the voice on his lap.

'Well, as sure as I can be,' said the talking kangaroo.

'I must say that there is one thing that puzzles me.'

'What?'

'Well, that voice is the voice of Inspector Speekup, right?'

Wilf nodded.

'Well, do you remember when the voice said, "And last, but not least, whatever Wilf is" and you said, "I'm a kangaroo". Do you remember that?'

'Of course I do, why?'

'Well, if you remember, the voice then said, "Are you? Well, whatever you are, you will enter last." Eh? Do you remember that?'

'Yes, but I still don't understand.'

'Well, I heard at the Black Bat Hotel that Inspector Speekup was as deaf as a post ...' They looked at each other for a moment. 'So, if the Inspector is so deaf ... how come he heard you say you were a kangaroo? Eh? How come?'

'You mean it's *not* the Inspector?'

'Right, and if it's not the Inspector who else can it be, other than Vernon, eh?'

'Great jumping kangaroos, you're right. Vernon's got them all in there and I'm next ...'

'Not quite ... let's say *we* are next. He doesn't know me and he can't see me either ...'

They both fell silent and waited for the door to open again.

*　　*　　*

Valentine looked at Vernon in his coffin for a full two minutes. Then, with sadness in his voice, he said, 'Oh Vernon, how different all this might have been if you had been as great a Vampire as your father was. You would be ruler of all of Gotcha now. How strange life is that I am President. But, even in death, I bear you no grudge although you were so cruel.'

Fifty feet up, in a swinging net, Valeeta had her hand over Victor's mouth so that he couldn't speak.

Valentine continued, 'Your mother and father loved you so much and had great plans for you. Goodbye Vernon, I wish you a good sleep.'

As he turned to go, Victor bit Valeeta's hand and she screamed with the pain. After all, a Vampire's bite can be very painful. The sudden noise made Valentine stop and look up. He couldn't quite make out what it was that was swinging so far above him. Vernon quickly took the false stake off his body and, before Valentine could see what was in the net, he hit him with it on his Presidential head. Valentine fell to the ground, knocked out cold.

'Not what I had in mind, but adequate.' Vernon dragged Valentine away from the coffin and rolled him under a bench and left him there. He looked up to his mummy and daddy.

'If you do that again,' he bellowed, 'not only will you watch the others die, but you will both watch each other die very, very slowly with a blunt stake.'

He sprang back into his coffin, fixed the stake and lay there with his foot on the pedal at the bottom of the coffin.

*　　　*　　　*

Wilf sprang around the room, muttering, 'Oh I wish I wasn't a kangaroo. I don't know how to handle myself as a kangaroo. Now, if I was a Werewolf, I would be able to get Vernon before he could get me.'

'Is there nothing you can do to turn yourself back?' The voice came from a jutting-out piece of rock.

'How do you mean?'

'Well, what if you really concentrated on being yourself again? It almost worked for me once. I really concentrated hard and, for almost an hour, my nose came into vision.'

'No, it doesn't work like that for Werewolves. We are activated by time. With me, it's the full moon.'

'But you're not a Werewolf, are you? You are a kangaroo and kangaroos are Australian, aren't they? Now the time in Australia is different from the time in Gotcha. In Australia, you would have to wait until tomorrow to turn into a Werewolf, wouldn't you?'

'You're too clever for me.'

124

'I know, but surely you can understand what I'm saying. Try concentrating. Keep telling yourself what the time is in Australia and see what happens. Go on, try, you've got nothing to lose. Have you, eh?'

'You're right. OK. I'm concentrating, I really am. By the way, what is the time in Australia, anyway?'

'Oh about ten hours ahead. It's about midnight here, so in Aussie land it'll be ten in the morning. Go on, hurry up and concentrate, you great, big antipodal.'

Wilf had no time to be offended. He crouched in a corner and thought hard about what time it was in Australia.

*   *   *

Vernon lay back with a big smile on his face that showed the two large teeth at the corners of his mouth. He lay there thinking, 'I've got Mummy and Daddy up there, swinging in the breeze. I've got Igon fast asleep and I've got my stupid brother knocked out cold under the bench. I'd better check he is asleep and give him an injection. If he were to come to while Wilf is here, it could prove a little awkward.'

He undid the wooden stake, humming a Vampirian air:

> *I'm a Vampire, aren't we all?*
> *Just a Vampire slim and tall.*
> *In my dreams I hear such lovely screams*
> *That I recall, but don't we all?*

He picked up a syringe that had been filled with K.O.D. (Knock-out-drops) and gently rolled Valentine's sleeve up above his wrist. With perfect aim, he found the vein and filled it with K.O.D. Valentine did not move and wouldn't for hours.

Vernon's mother looked down and saw what her wicked son was doing to his brother. She thought, 'Well, the rest will do him good.'

Fortunately for Wilf, all this activity had given him the extra time he needed hopefully to change back into either a Werewolf or his normal self. At the moment it seemed to be working. He really was concentrating hard and he wasn't a kangaroo any more. He was now a wallaby.

Wilf felt that he was winning and Mr C Menott was a great help with all sorts of encouraging words like, 'come on, you big dope, you can do it' or 'what's the matter with you, you hairy twerp?' Wilf felt that these words did help him to concentrate, but they were also words that he wouldn't easily forget; he would have to get Mr C Menott at least to say he hadn't meant them.

*　　*　　*

Vernon pressed his foot down on the door release and heard the door open once again. He did a quick check on his mother and father swaying above him and gave a quick look towards the outstretched bodies of Igon and Valentine who were in the Land of Nod.

He looked down at himself to see if everything was all right and he suddenly noticed that he had forgotten to put the false stake in position. Quick as a flash, he stamped hard on the door-close button and, as he tied the stake into its position, heard the door creak shut.

*　　*　　*

Wilf was doing his best and thanked the good Lord for reshutting the door as he still wasn't quite right, although he was no longer a kangaroo. He was no longer a wallaby either. He was something very pretty – he was a koala bear. A very large, but very pretty, koala bear.

'Keep going, Wilf, you're winning. You're a koala bear.'

'Really?' Wilf asked. 'But am I pretty?'

'The prettiest thing I've ever seen.'

Wilf seemed pleased and tried to concentrate harder. He groaned and grunted and Mr C Menott watched as Wilf's big, black nose changed shape and colour.

He shouted encouragement: 'Good old Wilf! Go, Wilf, go!'

Wilf went. He went from a koala to a very quick platypus then, all of a sudden, he was Wilf again. He looked down at his hands and feet.

'I did it, I did it!' he shouted to Mr C Menott.

'You certainly did, Wilf, but you're not as pretty as you were.' He smiled, but no-one saw him smile, so he told Wilf, 'I'm smiling, Wilf.'

'I wouldn't know. I wonder why the door closed again. But I'm glad it did. It gave me enough time, the time I needed. I would have felt such a fool going in there as a platypus.'

*   *   *

Vernon once more sprang into his coffin and checked that his stake was firm and real-looking. He knew that Wilf, whatever he was, was as sharp as a tack and as bright as a button. There were no flies on Wilf, except when he was a Werewolf on a hot day. Vernon's foot did its job and opened the door.

'Wilf the Werewolf, will you please enter.'

Wilf looked at where he thought Mr C Menott might be and smiled.

From the opposite direction a voice said, 'I'm here, Wilf, good luck!'

Wilf straightened his cravat and walked in. The door slowly closed behind him. For a moment Wilf couldn't see very well but, like all the others, after a few minutes he could see perfectly.

He walked to the candlelit coffin and tentatively peered in. He saw Vernon skewed and a big smile came to his face as he said out loud, 'Well, well, well, at last. At last someone, somehow has got rid of you, and about time. You have been the most hated man in the whole country. Not the county, but the country. All the time I knew you, I never met anyone who liked you one little bit. You were cruel, mean and not very nice.'

Here Wilf stopped for a second, as he was distracted by the buzz of a small housefly, nothing very magnificent, just an ordinary housefly. It flew around Wilf in circles, eventually landing on Vernon's long straight nose.

Wilf watched fascinated, as it slowly made its way along the nose towards Vernon's forehead, stopping every second or two, seemingly to sharpen its two front legs. He was going to swat the fly away, but he thought he saw something move which he felt shouldn't move, not when someone is supposed to be dead. It was only slight, so he waited and watched as Vernon's eyes slowly seemed to cross, as the fly made its tickling way along and up to the forehead. The eyes were now beginning to moisten from the effort of looking across at each other ...

'You're not dead, are you?' said a knowing Wilf.

Vernon still tried to play the part of the dead Vampire, not moving a muscle other than two hard-to-control wet eyes. Wilf put his hand out slowly to touch the stake which was piercing Vernon's heart. The two eyes uncrossed and looked down to where the stake was sticking out of the left hand side of his immaculate evening dress. As Wilf's hand came into contact with the stake it wobbled, rather like a loose tooth.

Wilf thought, 'That shouldn't be. If that stake had pierced the heart, it should be firm, but it's loose.'

He put his hand around the wooden stake, gripped firmly and tried to pull it. It held. He pulled again, harder this time, hard enough to lift Vernon into an almost-sitting position. He looked at Vernon's eyes as he held him sitting up. Vernon, always the supreme actor, still played dead dog.

Wilf took the pillow out of the coffin and, putting all his strength into it, he hurled Vernon back into a lying position. Vernon hit his head with an almighty whack on the wooden base of the coffin. Not only did his eyes cross but they shut, opened and shut again. A slight moan of pain came through his right lips. This time Wilf was certain.

'Vernon, you aren't dead. Where are the others?'

For the first time, Vernon allowed himself to become undead. He rubbed the back of his large Vampirian head.

Victor and Valeeta shouted down to Wilf, 'Vilf, Vilf, help us. Ve are trapped up here in dis net!'

'We are just above you.' Valeeta waved as Wilf looked up. He grabbed hold of the swinging rope. Victor panicked, 'Don't touch that rope, Vilf. Ve vill fall out.'

Vernon slowly crept out of his coffin and, while Wilf had hold of the rope, he quickly grabbed it and untied it. His mother and father screamed as the net suddenly dropped. They clung on to the net in mid-air, and Vernon laughed as he watched them swinging fifty feet above them.

Wilf, who was still hanging on to the rope, felt himself slowly rising upwards. The weight of their two bodies was easily pulling the weight of his one body up over the pulley. He knew that if he let go, they would come crashing down to the stone floor with a splat and a splot, probably a lot more splat than splot. So being a good, as well as a brave man, he held on. They passed each other about twenty-five feet up, Victor and Valeeta slowly dropping to the ground while Wilf slowly went up.

Vernon, with tears of joy in his vicious black eyes, grabbed the rope and held it for a second while he looped it round and through a ring handle on the floor. He knotted it tightly and looked up to see all three of them stuck twenty-five feet above him. Vernon knew that soon the rope would burn their hands and all three would hurtle to the floor, split, splat.

He danced with happiness, shouting, 'Come on down. The floor isn't very hard.'

As they looked down, all three of them knew that the least that they would get away with would be a broken leg each. Valeeta was the first who started to slip. Victor put one arm around her, begging her to hold on.

'I'm waiting,' Vernon laughed.

He ran over to Igon and slapped his face. 'Wake up, Igon. Wake up and see them fall!'

He didn't see the knot on the rope undo itself.

'Grab the net, Wilf!' a voice shouted.

Wilf needed no second telling. He swung the rope with all his strength and grabbed the net. All three of them were now hanging on to it. The loosened rope was somehow being held taut as the three of them were slowly, and somehow invisibly, let down to the floor.

When they were about three feet from the floor Wilf heard a voice say, 'You'd better jump, I can't hold on much longer.'

Wilf jumped and landed on the floor, grabbed the rope, and helped Mr C Menott ease the other two to the floor.

'Am I glad not to see you,' Wilf said.

Vernon had watched all this with an incredulous look on his face, while he still slapped Igon on the cheek although not with any power, just an automatic slap as he watched and heard Wilf talking to himself. His mother and father were in a state of collapse. Igon was still out cold, as was Valentine, who at one stage had woken up under the bench but, not knowing he was under a bench, had stood up quickly and knocked himself out again.

Vernon let Igon's head fall back on to the slab and, in a furious temper, pulled the strap that was holding him to the slab two notches tighter, across his chest, almost breaking Igon's ribs. He walked to his parents and to Wilf.

'You're very clever, Wilf, very clever indeed. I've always thought you were smarter than the others. But what's this habit of talking to yourself? That's a new one, isn't it? I thought only children did that, children and very old people,' he sneered at Wilf.

'You forget, Vernon, I'm a very old child. At least, I'm still a baby to my mother and, when I'm a Werewolf, I'm a very old one.' He seemed never to be afraid of Vernon and this always made Vernon regard Wilf with some admiration.

'You know, all of you, that I could kill you with one snap of my fingers. I could create magic that would astound you, even you, Father.'

Vernon's father was having difficulty untying some rope which was entwined around his arms and legs and which was making him stand in a crouched position on one leg. Valeeta was doing her best to help but she was in a weak state and was really of no help at all.

'Allow me,' Vernon said with a touch of sarcasm in his voice. 'Watch this, Wilf,'

He pointed to the rope and what seemed like a powerful light left his forefinger and hit the rope around Victor. After a few movements of his hand, the rope was lying limp on the floor.

Vernon smiled at Wilf, as if to say, 'Don't challenge me.'

Wilf smiled back as if to say, 'I have more up my sleeve than my arm,' hoping all the time that Mr C Menott was still around and willing to help. He was around and was standing behind Wilf.

He whispered very softly into Wilf's ear, 'You say, "watch this", then point to Igon.'

Wilf nodded. 'Watch this, Vernon.' He pointed at Igon and an amazed Vernon, and an amazed Wilf, watched as Mr C Menott undid all the straps holding Igon to the slab. Unfortunately Igon was still dreaming sweet dreams, so he couldn't be of any help.

'May I ask what you intend to do with us, Vernon?' Valeeta asked her son.

'Yes, Mother, you may. Go ahead and ask.'

'I just did.'

'Very well, I'll tell you, Mother dear.'

'Thank you, Vernon,' she replied.

'You are going to die.'

'Is that all?' his mother laughed. 'I thought you had something serious in mind.'

'I am serious. You're going to die, all of you.' He was starting to shout.

'Vill you please not shout at your mother. Vere did you learn these terrible manners?' Victor shouted.

'I'm sorry,' Vernon replied meekly, like a small schoolboy.

'That's all right. Now carry on, you vere sayink you vere serious ant you vere goink to kill us, all of us.' Victor smiled at his son.

'Yes.'

'How?' he asked.

'Slowly,' Vernon said thoughtfully.

'I think your father means how. You know, dear, *how* are you going to kill us, er, in what manner?' Valeeta smiled at her son.

'Well, I thought you and Dad should be skewed.'

'I hope the stakes will be sharp?' Victor asked.

'I'm sure they will. They were the best I could get. But the prices since I've been away in that statue! They've shot up.'

'Valentine?' asked Wilf.

'Oh, nothing special for him. I thought poison, a three-day one. The one there's no antidote for. That's risen in price, too.'

'What about me?' Wilf grinned.

'Ah, well, yes, I have something special for you, Wilf. You see, if you had been a Werewolf, I was going to roast you on a spit and, if you weren't a Werewolf, I was still going to roast you on a spit.' Vernon laughed – well, if you could call the throat noises he made, a laugh.

'You should have captured me when I was a turkey.'

'A turkey? You were a turkey?' said a smiling Vernon.

'Yes, just once.' Wilf was trying to keep any form of conversation going, until Igon and Valentine came round and saw what was going on and could help him. He continued, 'Then, in spring, I was a rabbit, then a kangaroo, then a wallaby and, for a few seconds, I was a platypus.'

'That's Australian, isn't it?'

'Yes,' Wilf nodded.

'How sad,' Vernon replied. 'You know, you haven't asked about Igon. I'm saving Igon till last.'

'You used to do that as a little boy,' his mother said. 'When you had anything special that you liked for dinner you used to save it till last, then eat it too quickly,' she reminisced.

Vernon looked at her with scorn and carried on as

if she hadn't spoken. 'As I was saying, I'm saving Igon until last. I've thought of something really good for him. First of all ... Wilf, would you like to sit down, are you getting tired?' Wilf shook his head. 'Well, Igon is going to be turned back into what he was! A filthy, ugly, toothless, slimy bunch of rags, then – now this is the best part – then I'm going to shoot him.'

'With a gun?' Wilf interrupted.

'With a cannon,' Vernon said proudly. 'Look!'

He pointed to the darkest corner and, with a swirl of his hand, lit up the whole area. They saw a huge cannon pointing upwards at the wall.

'Watch!' Vernon said proudly.

He closed his eyes tightly for a second and, in that moment, part of the wall moved open like a window. They saw the sky, then it closed. Vernon was beaming with the thrill of it all.

'I'm going to shoot him from that cannon. I have invented such a powerful gas that I can shoot him to the stars. The ignition is the difficult thing to do, but I've mastered that. So the next thing is to turn him back by doing the opposite to what you did, Father, when you turned him into what he is now. If I reverse the process, he will go back to his old horrible self. Then into the cannon and, pow, he's off to the stars!'

They all stood in complete silence. Valeeta was the first to speak.

'You always saved the glacé cherry on top of your ice-cream till last.'

'Mother, would you like to see the stakes?' Vernon asked, with hatred in his voice.

'No, thank you, dear. You were very fond of lamb

chops, but not very fond of steaks...'

Victor put his arms around his rambling wife. 'There, there, dear, don't worry. Everythink vill turn out vell.'

CHAPTER 10

Has Vernon won or lost the fight?
One way to tell is the sky at night.

Mr C Menott had been all round Vernon's lab and he had listened to all the conversations. It was obvious that neither Valentine nor Igon would be awake within the next hour, if not two. And Vernon had all the power on his side.

They couldn't kill him with anything other than a stake and he wasn't going to allow that to happen. His magic was all – powerful. It made the kind of magic that Victor did look like a magician's amateur night. But the thing that was on their side was Mr C Menott, because neither Vernon, nor anyone else for that matter, could see him. That made him a powerful ally.

For quite a while he had been looking very hard

and with great interest at the cannon. He stood directly in front of Wilf, looked at Vernon and spoke in a voice as near to Wilf's as was possible for him to imitate.

'How do you fire such a magnificent gun, then?'

Vernon looked at Wilf. 'That was clever. That really was clever, Wilf. Your lips – they didn't move when you spoke. How did you do that?'

Mr C Menott spoke again in Wilf's voice, this time saying, 'You show me how you're going to fire the cannon and I'll show you how to speak without moving your lips, OK?'

Vernon smiled. 'By all means.'

They all walked over to the cannon. The light shone in Vernon's eyes. It was obvious he was willing to talk about the gun he had invented.

'You see, in this cylinder here is a formula of gas that is really powerful. Just one drop could shoot a cannonball at least five hundred miles.' He looked at his captives as if waiting for applause but, as none was forthcoming, he continued.

'Now in this,' he held up the cylinder, 'is enough fuel to send a cannonball, or a man,' he pointed to the sleeping Igon, 'far and away beyond the moon.'

He dropped the cylinder on to the floor. Victor threw his arms around his wife to protect her from the explosion while Wilf's eyes widened to the size of saucers and his hair stood completely on end. Vernon laughed and laughed as he bent down to pick up the cylinder.

'It's perfectly safe. It can't go off on its own. It has to have heat. You see this cord in the base of the cylinder? Well, you have to pull that out about an

140

inch, then light it. The flame runs along the cord and melts the protective shield. Once that shield is melted, the heat ignites a vapour of inflammable gas. This gas is many degrees hotter than the first flame and that ignites the fuel store at the top end of the cylinder. There's about two pints.' He shook the cylinder and watched Wilf's hair move to an upright position again.

'Don't worry, Wilf, I promise you it can't go off unless it's lit.' He put the cylinder on the bench by the cannon.

'All you have to do is put it in the breech of the gun. Once in there, you lock it down and you light it. Then, whoof, off it goes and whoever's in there whoofs off with it . . .'

Vernon was talking as if he were giving a lecture at the Town Hall. Gone was the hatred of the people around him. If any one of them had put his hand up, he would have nodded as if to say, 'What is your question, Sir?' But no-one did, so he carried on, as if there were going to be questions later.

'It takes about twenty seconds for the heat to get through and maybe twenty-five seconds before the actual whoof . . .'

Mr C Menott had by this time looked everywhere, into every nook and cranny. He was now standing beside the enormous cannon, looking hard at the fuse that caused the whoof.

The problem as far as Mr C Menott was concerned was how to get dear old Vernon into the muzzle of the cannon. He jumped down unseen and made his way over to Wilf, tripping over what seemed like a bunch of eagle feathers and an undressed eagle next to them, looking as if it was waiting for its cleaning to be returned.

Mr C Menott looked hard at the bird and realized it was dead. He picked it up by its neck and twirled it around in the air, letting go of it rather like a hammer thrower. It shot out of his hands towards Vernon, who was still talking to everyone who could hear him, about how clever he was. Out of the corner of his eye he saw a naked eagle flying. No, the bird was not flying, it was spinning towards him.

Wilf moved as the large eagle zoomed low over his head on its way to its destination. Vernon watched with a surprised look on his face, trying to figure out how the bird could be flying, spinning or whirling towards him.

Valeeta, with a true mother's love, shouted to her son, 'Duck!'

While her husband looked at her and shouted, 'Eagle!'

The undressed thing hit Vernon with a resounding thwack, knocking him over.

Wilf cheered, shouting, 'He's been given the bird.'

The bird, which weighed a good thirty or maybe forty pounds, was lying limply across the chest of our fallen villain. Panic overtook Vernon and, amidst shouts of 'Get it off!', he tried to make it to his feet.

By the time he had, Mr C Menott had whispered quickly to Wilf, 'Give me a hand, Wilf.'

Wilf needed no second telling. He quickly made his way to the cannon, the bird and Vernon. Vernon was struggling with the wretched bird, but it wouldn't leave him. He couldn't get it off. It clung to him like glue. Vernon, of course, didn't realize that the eagle

was being well and truly helped by an invisible force.

Mr C Menott, who was finding it hard to hold the bird for any length of time, shouted, 'Wilf! Press the button to open the cave wall so that the cannon is pointing to the sky.'

Now to Vernon this looked as if the dead eagle was talking to Wilf. He used all his strength, threw the big bird off and ran, but Mr C Menott tripped him up.

Wilf shouted, 'That's what I want you to do when we play Gertcha!'

Vernon couldn't believe any of this. He watched from the floor as Wilf pressed the button that opened the cave wall. His eyes filled with angry tears as he

saw Valentine slowly waking up. He ranted at Wilf.
He pointed his hand at his father.

Mr C Menott saw Vernon's eyes change almost to
red in colour. He knew what Vernon was going to do.
Through his tremendous magic, he was going to set
fire to his father but, before the beam left his finger,
Mr C Menott pushed the arm firmly round. The
beam shot out and hit the door, smashing it to smith-
ereens with a very big explosion.

Vernon was now a complete madman, not under-
standing anything any more. He grabbed his mother
and held her in front of him, backing slowly to the
cannon.

'I'm taking her with me,' he snarled.

'Where are we going, dear?' his mother asked
gently.

'To the stars, you silly fool,' he snapped back. 'You
and I are getting into that cannon and we are going
to be shot into the sky, straight into space.'

'Oh now nice,' Valeeta smiled. She was still in a
state of shock and really didn't understand what was
going on.

Poor old Victor tried his best to draw on his magic,
but it was no good. He was so out of condition that,
when he drew a deep breath to prepare himself, the
only thing that happened was he became quite dizzy.

Igon was still lying on the table, feeling quite poorly
and wondering where he was. Valentine was feeling
the top of his head and wondering where the two
large bumps had come from. Wilf the Werewolf
looked round the room at his friends and quickly
realized that none of them would be able to help him.
It was up to him and the great Mr C Menott.

The quick-thinking Mr C Menott realized that, if anything was to be done, Wilf was the only person he would be able to rely upon. He weighed up the situation and, invisibly as well as instinctively, made his way to the cannon. He had to get there before Vernon.

However, Vernon got there first, still holding his rather bewildered mother in front of him as a shield. He had been very rough with Valeeta as he dragged her to the cannon, pulling her backwards.

The bewildered old lady spoke to her eldest son. 'Vernon,' she said, 'I don't think I care for this dance.'

Vernon's tongue lashed his mother as they stood by the cannon. 'Shut up, you oaf. You are a stupid woman.'

This was too much for Victor. He rose to his correct height and at the same time held in his tummy, saying, 'Vhy does he talk to his mummy like that? Vhy? Vere has he learnt all those bad sayinks?'

Vernon looked at his father and delivered another verbal lashing. 'You, too, are a fool. You are gross, fat like a pig. I'm ashamed of you, you silly, stupid man.'

As he was saying these terrible things, he put out his free arm and pressed a button. The barrel of the cannon slowly began to descend. It came to rest facing the ground. The muzzle of the cannon was large, over three feet in diameter, easily large enough for him to put his mother inside and to ram her down with the rammer; it was also long enough in the barrel for him to climb in after her. He only had to get her inside, rush round and light the fuse, then rush back and climb in, while at the same time pressing the button to raise the barrel to face the heavens.

As long as Wilf kept his distance it would be easy, but if Wilf started to cause him any problems, then the cannon would go off before it was in position, facing the heavens. He might be sent straight into the wall of the cave. He didn't relish the thought of that as he was to be first out of the cannon, and the power he had built into the cannon would send him against the wall at such a terrific speed that he would have a headache for a week.

Mr C Menott also knew what he had to do. He had to rescue Vernon's mother, push Vernon into the cannon, ram him down, light the fuse, face the cannon upwards and watch as Vernon sped towards the heavens and beyond even the Great Dracula. He looked sharply at the situation. Igon was once again asleep. Valentine was still groggy. The old King was, for the moment, useless and the ex-Queen was captured. He sprang to action. He stood directly behind Vernon. He shouted to Wilf.

'Wilf, light the fuse!'

Wilf needed no second bidding, except that as he ran to the cannon and jumped up to where the fuse was placed, he suddenly realized he had nothing to light it with.

He felt in all his pockets as Mr C Menott shouted, 'Light the fuse, Wilf. Come on, don't waste time. Light it, hurry.'

Wilf jumped down from the cannon and ran towards Igon who was fast asleep. He grabbed him and shook him, shouting, 'Matches! Have you got any matches?'

Igon slept on.

Vernon was now forcing his mother's head into the barrel of the cannon, much to the annoyance of his father.

Victor looked on, shouting, 'Don't go in there, mine little snowdrop!'

Suddenly Wilf was on to him. 'King Victor, have you got a light?'

'A light what?' ex-King Victor asked.

Wilf left him, hearing the cries of Mr C Menott. 'Please hurry, Wilf, or it will be too late.'

'I am hurrying,' Wilf shouted back.

He pounded on Valentine. 'I beg you, have you any matches?'

Valentine looked straight at him, but with unseeing eyes, oblivious to anything that was going on around him.

'It's no good,' Wilf shouted to Mr C Menott. 'I

can't get any matches.'

By this time Vernon was pushing his mother further into the cannon.

She spoke sharply to her son, 'Vernon, this is a very small and very dark room you're putting me into.'

'Get in, you silly old woman.'

'Your mother is not silly,' Victor shouted.

Mr C Menott did the only thing he could do. He grabbed Vernon from the back and started to tickle him. Vernon, who couldn't see who was tickling him, tried to whirl round but Mr C Menott hung on, tickling for all he was worth.

Vernon was very annoyed at first, but soon he was smiling, and soon after the smiling came the laughing, and after the laughing came near-hysteria. He was soon writhing on the floor with tears rolling down his cheeks as Mr C Menott tickled and shouted, 'Matches, who's got any matches? Give me some matches!'

Vernon, who thought he was the one being spoken to, shouted through his laughter, gulping for air, 'Stop, oh, oh, oh please, haha haha. No, don't, ha ha ha ha. Oh dear, ha ha, please, I beg, ha ha ha, you, oh oh, to sthahahaop. The matches are, ha ha ho ho, in haha, my, hohohoh hahah, top pock hahah, et.'

'Wilf,' shouted Mr C. 'The matches are in his top pocket. You get them. I'll keep tickling him.' And tickle he did, as Wilf got the matches.

Ex-Queen Valeeta was left to her own devices as she slid out of the cannon to the floor, saying, 'That room is too small. How could anyone throw a party in a room that size?'

She looked at Vernon writhing around the floor,

shouting, 'Oh stop, ha ha ha, please, oh oh, stop!'

The ex-Queen rose from the floor and looked at him. 'You are getting like your father. You drink too much.' So saying, she swept majestically across to her tired-looking husband.

'Take me home, Victor,' she commanded.

'Ya, mine little cowslip.' They made their way to the smashed door.

Wilf lit the fuse and said very quickly, 'It's done, it's lit.'

Mr C Menott said in a loud voice, 'Help me to put him in the cannon and hurry, we've only got a few seconds left before the cannon fires.'

Wilf helped him lift the now almost-exhausted Vernon into the cannon.

'The button, press the button that raises the cannon, Wilf.' This Wilf did, and slowly, very slowly, the barrel of the cannon rose and pointed to the stars.

The explosion that the cannon made was so loud that Chief Inspector Speekup, who was still sitting nervously behind his desk, said, 'Come in', twice.

Valentine and Igon sat bolt upright from the shock-waves and neither of them slept properly for the next two weeks.

Victor and Valeeta were caught in the turbulence and were more than ten miles past their home before they could land.

Mr C Menott was never heard again. One can only hope he was made visible.

Wilf never turned into a Werewolf again. Every full moon he turned instead into an Eleraffe, which, as everybody knows, is an elephant with a very long neck.

So once more Vernon was foiled. Once more good triumphed over evil. Although Valeeta never spoke of her son Vernon again, Victor was always looking up towards the sky at night. Once, he was with some-one who saw a falling star.

He turned to Victor and said, 'Look, a falling star.'

Victor looked up and waved, saying, 'That's not a fallink star. That's mine son, Vernon.'

He smiled.

THE END

PS Gotcha beat Gertcha one nil. 'The crowd looked silently on as the ball seemed to make its own way into the net. And five Gertcha players fell down when no-one was near them.'

(extract from *The Gotcha Nightly Express*)

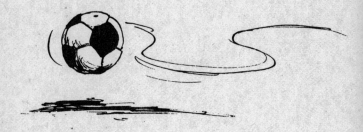

*Also by Eric Morecambe
in Magnet Books ...*

The Reluctant Vampire

'I don't like blood. I like chips and a small glass of red wine.' The Vampire Prince's shocking announcement begins a fantastic tale of ghoulish intrigue, spooky spells and hilarious horror!

'Slapstick dialogue and ghoulish goings-on . . .'
The Mail on Sunday

'Lots of typical Eric laughs for sevens and eights – and the rest of the family if they can get hold of it for long enough . . .'
Mother Magazine

'Sparkling and spooky . . . full of wit and word-play . . .'
Lancashire Evening Post